Big Deuce
The Tom Dreyfus novels

My Sweet Lorraine
&
Jake Leg

Written by
Mike McCune

©
Copyright 2014
Worldwide Rights Reserved

Big Deuce the Tom Dreyfus novels *My Sweet Lorraine & Jake Leg*

FIRST EDITION

Written by Mike McCune © Copyright 2014 –
Original draft © Copyright 2005, Mike McCune, Big Deuce, the Tom Dreyfus novels: My Sweet Lorraine & Jake Leg
© Copyright 2000, Mike McCune, My Sweet Lorraine

Editor-in-Chief: Steve William Laible, MBA

KodelEmpire.com (info@kodelgroup.com)

Published by The Kodel Group, LLC
PO Box 38 - Grants Pass, Oregon 97528

Imprint: Empire Holdings

Copyright © 2014 Mike McCune. All Rights Reserved and protected under the 1976 Copyright Act and the Pan American and International Copyright Conventions. The reproduction and distribution of this publication without the prior written consent of the publisher, is illegal and punishable by law "except" in the case of brief quotations embodied in critical articles and reviews. Names, characters and incidents depicted in this story are of the author's own expressions.

Summary: Set in Los Angeles in 1946, My Sweet Lorraine is a story of corruption, passion, loyalty, and a homicide detective's biggest mistake: assumptions. In 1949 Tom Dreyfus and his partner, Munson are back in Jake Leg to investigate a series of murders.

Library of Congress cataloging-in-publication data: McCune, Mike. Detective Fiction.
Library of Congress Control Number: 2014932891

ISBN: 978-1-62485-008-0
eBook ISBN: 978-1-62485-009-7

Printed in the United States of America, Europe, Asia and beyond...

To my father, Jack

And to my sons, Jim and Dan

With love

In memory of Elmore Leonard

Thank you, Melissa

[signature]
May 2014

My Sweet Lorraine

Prologue

Searchlights along Sunset Boulevard swayed like palm trees in a Santa Ana wind, beckoning GIs and sailors home. Back pay burning holes in their pockets, vets didn't need to look hard for ways to play catch-up: there was a clip joint, pimp, or shill on every Hollywood street corner just waiting for a sucker with a fat wallet. At the Coconut Grove the jazz was hot, the booze flowed, and any "Joe" could rub elbows with Cooper, Gable, or Lombard. Work could wait. In 1946 Los Angeles was jumping around the clock.

It happened on a hill overlooking a Gomorrah with lights enough to rival the stars.

He'd slumped in a corner awaiting the Kingdom when headlights pierced the darkness of his basement room. A car screeched to a halt, its doors slammed, then came arguing from the driveway.

Damn. Dem' bitches said they'd be out all night.

He carefully drew the spent needle from his left forearm and unclenched his fist, let go the end of rubber surgical tube with his teeth. The shaking stopped cause he'd be rushing soon, the horse racing. Groping, he began to tidy up.

"Be cool, be cool, they think you're jammin' at the Mamba."

The arguing from the driveway didn't stop. It got louder . . .

"What-'da-fuck?"

He just had to work himself up to the filmy basement window and see. Though it was hard to see straight he could tell, "Salt n' Pepper all right." He could hear the cat fight.

"Can't leave it alone, can you bitch? A man? A man!" the black one said.

"So? They're my business," the white one answered.

"You're *my* business. Business used to be good."

"I don't know what you're talking about."

"No? Well I'm done *talkin'*, bitch."

From his darkened pit he saw the tire iron come down hard and fast in the high beams. Again and again "Pepper" brought it down on the fallen girl who was long past caring. He saw the big sister pick up the limp one and dump her in the trunk, then pour gas over the gumbo on the concrete and light a match. Numb, he watched the car speed away, its headlights slicing through the night. *That's funny* he thought, *the driveway's on fire*. He'd reached the Kingdom far too late. Invisible, all he could do was slump back down in his corner, scrunch his knees to his chest, wrap his arms around them tight, rock back and forth and whimper "Oh, man."

Chapter 1

Over my loudspeakers there was that soft, monotonous "hiss-pop, hiss-pop" a stylus makes when it hits a record label and you don't do anything about it. Under the spell of this Monday lullaby I snored in my easy chair, sporting a thirty-six-grit beard and breath that reeked of the kraut dog I ate yesterday. The scene was nothing new to any fly on my ceiling: the sports page in a heap on the floor – this morning's headline, **'CITATION' WINS TRIPLE CROWN** – a finished solitaire game spread on the coffee table alongside an empty rocks glass, an empty fifth of bonded bourbon, with an overflowing ashtray riding sidecar. The cards that had been in my hand the night before lay spilled in my lap like flotsam. Just as well, after turning over the deck a dozen times I hadn't been able to show the black queen I was looking for –

The phone rang reveille and I snapped-to with a four-alarm hangover. Mornings were definitely getting tougher cause the long haul to kill the ringing seemed uphill. Took no soothsayer to know who was on the other end, my ex-wife never called unless I was late with an alimony payment and that was mailed three days ago. I distinctly remember the "Up Yours" I'd penned in the memo section of the check.

"Munson?"

"Where-the-hell you been? I've been trying to reach you all morning."

"Busy. I'm on vacation, remember?"

"Vacation's over. Got us a sweet little homicide here and the Chief says we're on it."

"Thought Sykes was on shift. Let Bingham put him on it."

"Can't, he's working another case. What else you got going, besides that hangover you're nursing?"

"Gimme a break." Munson was right, I was tired of arranging my spice rack in alphabetical order, and the weekend benders were taking a toll . . . "Make it the short version, okay?"

"1750-C West Adams. Got a call around 7:20 from a June Rutledge – secretary on her way to work. Said she smelled a stink coming from her neighbor's bungalow, rented by a Lorraine Jardine. Boys got there half-hour ago and found Miss Jardine on the bathroom floor with her face bashed-in and a photo alongside what's left. She's been dead at least two days. Photo checks-out with the landlord, it's the victim all right – cute as silk panties – least she was . . . There's a handbag near the body, but no one's touched it; sealed-off the place so no press can get through; questioned most of the neighbors. So far no one saw or heard a thing. Rutledge dame says Jardine kept to herself, they chit-chatted a couple of times."

"About what?" I asked, massaging my aching head.

"She can't remember."

I checked my watch. It read 9:40. "All right Munc, give me half an hour and stay with the landlord."

*   *   *

A strip of manicured lawn as flat as a putting green split two rows of stucco bungalows with roofs of terra-cotta tile. Bougainvillea, bird of paradise, and rhododendron flanked the bungalows, flowers outnumbering leaves ten-to-one. As I pulled-up to the curb of the Adams Arms I could see Munson leave a slender, bald-headed guy standing with his hands on his hips and make his way past the cordon. He was holding what looked to be a fistful of receipts that he held out to me as I got out of my Buick Roadmaster.

"Jeez Tom, she's paid a year's rent in advance, *in cash*."

"Bald guy the landlord?" I asked, not reaching for the mangled paper in Munson's fist.

"Yup. Name's Bernard."

"Swell."

As I approached him, Bernard looked like a boil about to pop. My head pounding like a weekend bowling alley, I put on my PR face and flashed the badge.

"Tom Dreyfus, Homicide. Sorry about the inconvenience." Bernard shook all over as he pointed at Munson.

"That man is a cretin!"

I looked over my shoulder, then back with a smirk. "Yeah, well finesse was never his strong suit. You told him Miss Jardine paid a year's rent in advance?"

"Yes, in cash."

"A little unusual?"

"What should I have done, return it and asked for a check? My tenants are carefully screened; this sort of thing has never happened here."

"I'm sure." I reached in my breast pocket and fished-out a business card. Bernard took it like it'd go off in his face. "You never know when you'll recall something. Now the sooner I get to my investigation, the sooner you can rent that bungalow."

The front door hadn't been jimmied but I turned to Munson anyway. "No forced entry, the windows or back door?" He checked his notes and shook his head. We spread Vicks Vapor Rub under our nostrils and entered.

Bernard must have killed the furnace cause the bungalow felt like a tomb. Shafts of blue light sliced through Venetian blinds that cast horizontal bars of shadow across the eggshell Berber carpet. Lorraine Jardine couldn't have spent much time at home, and when she had she wasn't expecting company: the only piece of furniture was a rocking chair, at the center of the living room, facing away from the window. Munson jotted some notes then we continued, up the hall, the rendered-fat stink nearly knocking us sideways. As we approached a sliver of light coming from the cracked bathroom door, flies droned. I tapped open the door with the eraser-end of my pencil . . . "Ah, Jeez!"

"You ain't gonna upchuck, are you Tom?"

"No, I ain't gonna upchuck." Damn near: There, on the cold tile, was a colder Lorraine Jardine, or so we'd confirm from her dental records. What had been her beautiful face was now pulp, with something resembling guacamole leaking out of her ears, the flies going for this. Incredibly, her jaw was intact but shoved to one side of the mashed face, and was smiling up at me as if to mock, "I know who killed me and you don't."

With his usual flair for understatement Munson responded, "Not a pretty sight."

"Yeah, so where's the blood?"

Munson tore his eyes from the corpse and noticed the clean bathroom.

"She was murdered somewhere else, then brought here." I nodded to the floor. "Someone's done a good job of erasing evidence, too . . . Get the camera, then lift me a clean set of prints."

"Tom, the landlord ID'd her from the photo."

"You kidding me? That could be Bess Truman for all we know."
"Not with those legs."
"Just *do* it. Okay?"

Munson shrugged and left for his car.

I watched him, then pulled my hip flask and took a stiff belt. Kneeling, I reached for the handbag with my handkerchief and shook-out its contents. Paper on tile can make a deafening sound: five hundred in cash, a matching withdrawal receipt from Security Mutual, and a folded handbill.

No lipstick, cosmetics, checkbook? This stuff's been planted.

"Shit." My guts still on fiddle strings, I took another slug from the flask and forced myself to look at the smiling pile of goo again: she was in a black and bloodied cocktail dress that hadn't been ripped or pulled up to her chest, nor the underwear pulled down around her ankles, with no traces of dried semen. On my way to the Adams Arms I'd checked, there were no priors on a Lorraine Jardine. A clothed body without a past, no signs of rape, with what had been done to her making too much noise for anyone within earshot to ignore? *What'd this dame seen, who'd she cross? What else besides money or sex was her killer after?* It was Chinese arithmetic, nothing added up. I was holstering my hip flask when the folded flier slapped me in the face. Munson had returned with the Speed Graphic and was loading a film back.

"Look at this" I called, and held up the unfolded handbill announcing a five-piece combo: **Inky and his Inkwells**, headlining through April at a joint called the Mamba Club. In the upper-third of the handbill was a photo of the combo where someone had scrolled in ballpoint 'Your Sugar Man,' above the piano player, a handsome young Negro.

"The Mamba Club?"

"Yeah, a dive in colored town."

Munson went back to his camera, loading a blue bulb into the bowl reflector of its flashgun. "So who's this Inky, and who's 'Sugar Man'?" he asked, shooting an angle of the corpse.

"Unless we lift a clean set of prints, or locate the car that brought her here, it's our only lead."

* * *

Our preliminary investigation over we called the morgue for the meat wagon, thanked Bernard for his cooperation then walked to our cars. It looked like rain.

When we'd stashed the gear I said, "Let's have a look at those rent receipts." Munson extracted the wad from his right-coat pocket and handed them to me. I needed both hands. "Twelve," was all he said as he held open the door to my Buick.

Slumping behind the wheel I unraveled the mess, examining each receipt before making a circle of them on the passenger seat. From my breast pocket I took out the photo of Lorraine Jardine and placed it at the hub of the configuration. Munson leaned in through the open passenger-side window, chewing his wad of Beemans as he watched.

Except for the dates the receipts were identical, each section meticulously filled-in with flawless penmanship as, I was sure, only Bernard could have, the lingering scent of his Bay Rum as good as a finger print. In the 'rent' section '$125.00' showed, the box checked 'cash' alongside it. In the section marked 'occupancy' the number 'one' was spelled-out.

Her bungalow has only one bedroom. So no one's registered as living with her, so what? A woman like that must've had lots of boyfriends. Why would someone want twelve separate receipts if they could pay a year's rent in advance? Or maybe Bernard's just the obsessive type.

The loud "smack-chick" from Munson's gum chewing brought me back.

"So what do you think, Tom?"

I scooped up the receipts and held them out to Munson, who reluctantly took them and began stuffing them back into his pockets. "I *think*, you should get back and develop those negs, check the print index, then wait for the results of the autopsy. I'll visit the Mamba Club and find out what I can about this Inky."

Munson nodded, turned and went to his car. I watched him peel away then make a U-turn in the middle of Adams Boulevard and head east, downtown.

Mike McCune

Chapter 2

Known to cops as "Billy Goat Acres," the city of Bell Gardens hugs Atlantic Boulevard like a tumor hugs a smoker's lung. Defense contracts took a nose-dive after the war and a lot of coloreds who'd made good money in the plants of south-central Los Angeles found themselves out of work and desperate. The worst fear of a white salesman making the rounds between Pasadena and Long Beach was to get a flat here. More than likely he'd abandon his car and hoof it out, pronto.

Finding the Mamba Club was easy; blindfolded, no one could miss a dive painted purple and yellow, and so conveniently sandwiched between a pawnshop and a liquor store. I swallowed and stepped in, the joint going as quiet as a graveyard in a snowfall. When my eyes adjusted to the dim light I headed for the bartender, this suave old dad who must've been something before the Civil War. As I shifted between the tables it felt like every eye in the place was looking for a soft spot to shove a shiv.

The smooth rim of the mahogany felt warm and comforting under my forearm, but the old bartender ignored me and kept on polishing the same rocks glass. "Excuse me, could we talk?" I asked, extracting the folded handbill from my breast pocket when a bouncer the size of a beer truck came from nowhere, crowding my right so close I couldn't tell whether it was my toes I was feeling or his.

"What you want, man, this here's a colored place. Ain't nothin' for you here, jus' do-the-scram."

I turned, craning way back to get a look at him. He was impressive: an easy six-foot five-inches, two hundred and fifty pounds, he eclipsed what little light was in the joint, had no neck and was as bald as an eggplant. His nose looked as if it'd been broken lots of times, with nothing smaller than a floor safe. "You a cop?" he asked. I showed him the badge.

"Detective. No shakedown, just a talk with the bartender."

"What for, he do somethin' wrong?"

"No. It's confidential."

"What if he don't wanna' talk to you?"

With a smile as warm as mother's milk, I opened my coat and made sure the bouncer got a long look at the .38 Special. "He will

– call it a hunch. Now unless you're waiting for me to ask you to dance?"

"Jimmy! Got us a smart-ass cop wants to see you."

The old bartender took his time, just to prove he was in control of the situation, but finally stood across the bar from me. To the bouncer I said, "Excuse us."

"I'll be all right, Sam," the bartender said.

Satisfied, Sam stuck a toothpick in the corner of his mouth and left as quietly as he'd come. The "hum" of conversation resumed, a woman laughed, someone put a dime in the jukebox and Billie Holliday's longing and pain floated amongst the smoke.

"So what you want, mister detective?"

"Answers to some questions, then I'll go. What can you tell me about these?" I asked unfolding the handbill and laying it on the bar in front of him, countering with the photo of Lorraine Jardine. A greenback with Andy Jackson's portrait seemed to jog the old bartender's memory.

"Never seen the white woman before – easy on the eyes, though." With an index finger he tapped the piano player on the handbill, smiled and shook his snowy head like a reminiscing father. "That there's Inky. They'd stand in his shadow just to get a bone. Man, could that boy shake them ivories."

"Did anyone call him 'Sugar Man'?" I asked, pointing to the ballpoint scroll.

"None I know."

"When was the last time you saw him?" The old bartender squared at me with an answer that paid-off in silver dollars.

"Bout' five days ago, when he come to collect their pay."

"Wait a minute." I held up the handbill. "This says the band's got another week left in their gig."

"Ain't no band; least, not no more. Done split after the owner fired their ass."

"Why?'

"Inky never showed for half their sets. Nigger's a junkie."

"Where's he live now?"

"Roun' Lennox, with his mother . . . Last name's *White*."

"You're kidding."

"Go figure," said the bartender. Satisfied the rocks glass was clean enough he shelved it.

A cocktail waitress the color of caramel leaned across the bar. She shot a glance at me and shrugged indifference. "Need a gin rickey and two ol' fashions, Jimmy." In a wink Jimmy poured generous, mixed, placed them on her tray and she was gone.

"So what about the rest of the band?"

"Like I says, they split. Drummer and bass landed a gig in New Orleans, tenor sax got one in Chicago, guitar player's a mechanic – used car lot somewhere on Figueroa."

"Do I need names, any priors?"

"Weren't punks if that's what your askin', jus' full of juice – drink hooch, smoke reefer, play music n' chase skirt's all. Ain't hurtin' nobody."

"Thanks," I said, rapping my knuckles on the bar as I left. I believed him.

Lennox is about ten miles southwest of the Mamba Club, as close to suburbs as most coloreds ever get. Though small, most of the homes are well kept, with postage-stamp lawns and a pruned tree or two – I'm familiar with the town only cause Hollywood Park's in its backyard. A Richfield service station phone book told me what I already figured, that there weren't many families with the last name of 'White' living in Lennox.

* * *

A rusty screen door separated me from the shadowed interior of a brown stucco house on Buford Street. The buzzer didn't work, no matter how many times I pressed it to convince myself it did. I was about to give up knocking when I heard the sounds of a toilet flush, a door open then slippers shuffle on Linoleum.

"Every God-damned time! Hold on, I'm comin'!"

"Mrs. White? Mrs. Selma White?"

"Who wants to know?" asked a colored woman who came into relief from behind the rusty screen door: in her early-forties with a lot of mileage. I caught myself staring. A lean five feet seven-inches at least, she was made taller by a neck that went on forever, punctuated by a goiter the size of a Vidalia onion. In a caftan with plumed collar she looked like a flamingo that'd swallowed an eight ball.

"State your business, ofay."

"... The name's Dreyfus, I'm looking for your son," I said, showing her the badge.

"*Homicide?* I kicked the pisser out – a leech, jus' like his ol' man."

Initially, you'd describe Selma White as 'less than concerned' over her son's whereabouts, but once you got past all that anger you'd still describe her as a *real mother.* I caught her looking past me and turned. An elderly neighbor was peering out her window from behind some curtains.

"Luella Turner, mind your business you old battle axe!" Satisfied, Mrs. White turned back. "So what's Inky done now?"

"Mind if I come in?" I asked, scratching at her screen door. "I feel like a mosquito out here."

Stepping from the porch and into Mrs. White's foyer was like stepping into the tropics, diffuse daylight filtering through a large, dirty window and softening peach-colored walls. It was Moorish: two archways, one leading to the bed and bath room(s), the other leading to the living area, faced north and east. Except for a single rattan peacock chair against the east wall, and a threadbare Moroccan rug, there were potted plants everywhere. The cloying atmosphere of the atrium made me jumpy.

"Nice," I said.

Languid and silent, Mrs. White led me past the east archway, to a tasteful if sparsely furnished living room, much darker, and cooler, than the foyer. Turning, I noticed a Baldwin upright piano with some framed photos on top. She gestured to a sofa then sat across from me on an old wing-backed chair, crossed her legs and lit a cigarette. I couldn't help thinking what a paradox the whole scene was, like a Bogart-Bacall flick angled a bubble-off plumb.

I cleared my throat. "Mrs. White, three days ago a young woman was murdered. We found the body in the West Adams district." She didn't bat an eye. "Your son isn't a suspect. I don't know if he witnessed the murder or knew her, but if he did I can help him. All we found next to the body were these." I unfolded the handbill on the coffee table between us then added the photo of Lorraine Jardine. She picked up the handbill, studied it then set it back down like it was a soiled diaper.

"Yeah, that's the club Inky was playin' fore he moved back home." She glanced past me, at the piano then stared down at her hands. "The boy has talent, a natural."

"What about the woman? Ever see her?"

She looked at the photo and shook her head. "No."

"Did anyone refer to Inky as 'Sugar Man'?"

"None I know."

"Where's Inky now?" She didn't look up.

"Some rescue mission downtown. Maybe they can do somethin' with him, I ain't got it in me no more."

I left my card on the coffee table and she showed me out. On my way past the piano, I got a closer look at a portrait of the three Whites – minus the father. In the portrait, to Mrs. White's left, was a beautiful . . . daughter? She looked to be about five years older than Inky.

I asked.

"Oh, that's Bonita. She's no good either."

I wish I'd paid more attention to her reply. Mrs. White closed the door behind me.

Mike McCune

Chapter 3

It was 2:30 and I hadn't had breakfast or lunch. After what I'd put my stomach through in the last seventeen hours it was time to treat it nice. Back in town I stopped at Nickodel's, ordered eggs Florentine and a Bloody Mary, then phoned Munson from the lobby. He was real sore about me having chased down our only lead solo.

"Objectivity, Tom," Munson pleaded. "What's the point of having a partner if you don't want his opinion?"

"Bunk," I said. Split, we'd covered twice the ground in half the time and he knew it. "You got the results of the autopsy?"

"Girl died three days ago, last Saturday round ten p.m. Place her age from nineteen to twenty-one. Had dinner, some booze, but no dope. She wasn't raped. No ligature marks or signs of her being gagged, so she probably knew her killer. The guy was right handed, strong and mad-as-hell. Cause of death was multiple blows to the head with a metal object – pipe or a tire iron. Postmortem shows her face was backed over by a car – Cooper tire."

"Jeez," I winced. "What about prints?"

"Perp wore gloves. One must've had a hole in the right index finger. We lifted a partial of an arch off the handbag, but it ain't enough to make our killer . . . There's something else, Tom"

"What?"

"Bingham. He was riding my ass with all kinds of questions about the investigation, like he's taking it personal. He wants you in his office, now."

"The guy pulls me from vacation to work a homicide, and what do I get? Where's fucking gratitude? All right, I'm grabbing a bite. Run a rap sheet on a Robert Jefferson White, AKA 'Inky,' then meet me at the City of Angels Rescue Mission on 13th Avenue."

" . . . Right."

When I got back to the booth my eggs Florentine was cold and the celery in my Bloody Mary had wilted.

The padre escorted Munson and me to the rec. room without saying a word, just shaking his head to himself. He gestured to the opposite wall then backed out without either of us noticing.

Our footsteps echoed as we crossed the parquet floor, to where a young Negro was kneeling in front of a battered upright piano. He looked about twenty. He looked like he was praying to the keys.

I cleared my throat . . . "Robert White? 'Inky?'" The opened badge hung limp in my hand as I introduced Munson and myself. The kid didn't budge. I glanced at Munson, who offered a shrug. "What're you doing, Inky?" I asked. The kid finally turned from the piano, grinning ear-to-ear like he'd been in the Sahara too long, his pupils dilated bigger than bull's-eyes.

"Sayin' goodbye to an ol' friend," Inky replied. "Nice set of teeth, huh?"

"He's stoned to the b' Jesus belt," Munson scoffed.

*   *   *

The padre explained that because Inky insisted on "flying higher than the Angels" he had to leave. Sure, his rap sheet showed he'd been busted numerous times for misdemeanors involving narcotics, but not once for a violent crime. If this penitent, piano-playing hophead fit the MO of a killer then I was Donald Duck. Munson and I were too potty trained; we frisked and cuffed him, then shoved him in the back of the Buick. Inky seemed grateful.

"He's a dead man if the killer finds out he witnessed the murder," I said to Munson at his car.

"We don't know if he saw anything."

"What else we got? Shit, Munc, we could put it in a thimble and have room to stir. Whatever the kid's seen he's connected, but we'll have to dry him out first. I say we get a gallon of coffee into him, take him to my place and let him go cold turkey. We can take shifts working the evidence. That'll give me time to pull that bug out of Bingham's ass."

Munson nodded, his way of saying 'I think it's a great plan.'

I fumbled in my breast pocket till I found the piece of paper I was looking for, handing Munson the Security Mutual receipt.

"Verify the withdrawal and who was on the account, I'll get him some coffee then meet you at my place."

"Right."

I could tell Munson saw it was right, as "right" as our only move could be.

*   *   *

Inky was shaky over the wait, that and the horse still in his bloodstream. I took him to Langer's Deli, un-cuffed him and offered to buy him lunch. "Ain't hungry," he said after we'd found a booth.

Inky lit a cigarette and looked around. "So dis' where white folks eat kosher."

I signaled Doris for two Java's. "This is the place," I answered and lit an overdue smoke for myself, unsure if a stopover at a public venue was smart.

Doris brought the coffeepot and filled two mugs. "Long-time-no-see, Tom. You boys want anything?"

"Just the coffees . . . and that date you keep promising me."

"Cute. My boyfriend would break off your arms and beat you to death with them."

Our usual repartee cut-off, Doris's jaw hit the table. I turned. Oblivious, Inky was pouring half the sugar dispenser into his mug, his hands shaking enough to generate a Richter reading. He brought the mug to his quivering lips and drained the scalding mocha syrup in a draft, slopping most of it down his front. We were drawing attention.

"What's with your friend?" Doris asked.

I shrugged a lie.

Feeling the weight of recriminating eyes, Inky snapped. "What'ch'all lookin' at? Never seen a man drinkin' coffee?"

"Easy," I countered with as much velvet as I could muster. "We'd better take the coffees to-go," I said to Doris, who hurried away like we had rabies.

I scooted out of the booth. "Get up." Inky looked up like a wounded cur, shaking violently.

"I don't need your help!"

Quick, I put my face in his. "I'm all you've got, so pull your pucker-string tight and find your knees." Inky stood awkwardly, bracing himself against the table, sweating profusely. Knowing he'd fall without help, knowing he had to get out of that place, he swallowed his pride and let me help him up the isle to the register. It was the longest five yards of my life.

It was raining hard when I got Inky out of Langer's, half-tripping over him as we stumbled our way back to the Buick, feeling like an idiot for bringing him here in the first place. By the time I poured him onto the back seat my only lead was going through the D.T.'s. Missing my step from the curb to the running board I stepped, ankle-deep, into the torrent frothing down the culvert in search of a drain. Soaked fedora-to-socks, behind the wheel I lost it –

"Mother fucking son-of-a-bitch!"

From the back seat, moaning softly in delirium came, "Don't beat me, *please,* don't beat me again, Daddy."

Chapter 4

My Florsheims "squished" as I entered the lobby, hefting the body toward the elevator. Nothing escaped Flora Riddle, my landlady. "Is everything all right, Detective Dreyfus?" she asked, peering from her cracked front door, rouged and looking embalmed, her skin as dry as a beached seal's. Mrs. Riddle read dime novels and I was her favorite tenant.

"Fine, Mrs. Riddle. Just a little homework," I replied, which must've looked odd since I was obviously having difficulty schlepping a comatose young Negro over my shoulders.

"He isn't dead, is he?"

"Not yet."

"Your partner arrived earlier," Mrs. Riddle called after me. "I let him in."

"Thanks," I said, lurching under Inky's weight and into the elevator. As the doors closed I imagined her: standing on her dining room table, her ear pressed to an inverted rocks glass against the ceiling. By tomorrow morning the nosy old hen would have a well-deserved crick in her neck.

Exhausted, I kicked at the door to my apartment. It opened quickly, Munson's face going stupid.

"Jeez Tom, you look like hell."

"Thanks very little," I said, lurching my way past him and toward the bathroom.

"What's that stink?"

"I think he pissed his pants. Get the handcuffs."

"Handcuffs?"

"He had the shakes in the car. If we don't get that shit out of him we'll lose our witness," I said, lowering Inky before the toilet. The kid lay in a heap on the tile.

I shucked my coat like it was on fire, then my tie and shirt, as Munson returned with the cuffs. "All right, get him in front of the john and snap them on, tight."

"You gonna drown him?"

"No, keep him from drowning." I fished around in the medicine cabinet while Munson wrestled with Inky.

"His pulse's pretty weak, Tom."

"We'll fix that." I showed Munson what I'd pulled from my medicine cabinet: "When I pop this ammonia stick he should come-to, then I'll pour this Ipecac down his throat. When the stuff kicks-in keep his head in the toilet, I'll hold him from the back."

Munson looked up, pleading. "You sure about this?"

I answered by snapping the ammonia stick under Inky's nostrils. The kid lurched, gulping for air like a catfish. I pinched his nose and poured the syrup down his throat. Inky thrashed, his strength amplified by delirium, but Munson managed to hold his head into the bowl as I jerked up on the cuffs. We felt him tighten, then saw the gush of yellow bile shoot from his mouth, followed by another, then another.

"Ah, shit!" Munson and I echoed in harmony. We held on.

Inky convulsed and puked his last offering. After that he was spent, collapsing in a fetal-tuck before the toilet.

I checked his pulse. Satisfied, I flushed the toilet then leaned back against the pedestal sink and lit a cigarette. Munson sat at the opposite corner of the bathroom, his elbows resting on his knees. "This kind of duty ain't in my job description," he said.

"He'd better have something to say when he comes to or swear-to-Christ I'll shove an ice pick in his ears."

"Save an ear for me."

We lifted Inky and carried him to the sofa. I wiped his mouth then took off his shoes, covered him with a blanket and left him snoring.

"I need a drink," I said, reaching the cocktail cart. Cracking the seal on a fifth of Old Grand Dad, I poured a double and handed it to Munson, keeping the bottle for myself.
"Watch our *witness* while I clean up."

When I stepped out of the bathroom I found Munson seated across from the sofa, smoking a cigarette and reviewing his notes. Two mugs of coffee were on the table. Inky lay on the sofa exactly as I'd left him, on his left side.

"He say anything?"

Munson looked up from his notes. "Not a peep." He took the last drag from his cigarette and crushed it out, nodding toward the mugs. "Made some coffee."

"Thanks," I said, and sat in my favorite easy chair, grateful Munson hadn't while I was showering – those little courtesies that cement a partnership. "So what about the bank withdrawal?"

Munson flipped over a page of his notepad. "Account's in Lorraine Jardine's name only. It doesn't mean she set it up. Whoever did, it was opened last January. Paperwork says she came from New Orleans; address of record's 'bungalow five' at the Adams Arms. Occupation's listed as 'clerical;' beneficiaries, 'none'."

"Great, she's a ghost. Anything else?"

"Boxcars. Four-and-five digit figures going in-and-out her account the whole time."

"She's a whore?"

Munson shrugged. "It's what the money says. High class, too. Sure as hell ain't no clerk."

His face went blank as he reached for his coffee mug, a sign Munson was holding back. "What?"

"I think she was making a break. That's why she was killed."

"Call girl making a break with five-hundred bucks?"

Munson shrugged again. "She spent a lot. And there's her pimp to think about."

"Maybe, but she's got no priors. Not here, not New Orleans, not anywhere."

"She crossed somebody. Unsolved files are loaded with broads come to Hollywood figuring they're the next Liz Taylor, then wind up turning tricks. One thing's sure, she's got family somewhere wondering where she is."

"Right," I said. Until now Lorraine Jardine was this svelte body minus a face. It never occurred to me she had a family. I looked at Inky. "He'll sleep like a rock and I need to report to Bingham. Can you watch him for a couple of hours?"

"Sure."

I got my coat. "Keep his head turned and keep him warm."

Munson nodded. "Kid's gotten to you, hasn't he?"

"I'll relieve you as quick as I can," I said and shut the door behind me.

It was 6:20 when I got to City Hall, the Red Cars making their final runs to Pico Boulevard. Homicide Division's on the ground floor, at a grassy knoll on the southeast corner of Spring Street and First. During the day, most of the detectives come-and-go through two large double-hung windows, but at night everyone checks-in through the lobby, past the desk Sergeant.

"How goes it, Mike?"

The desk Sergeant put down the sports page for the six syllables. "Hey, Tom! Pretty quiet tonight." My heels echoed as I angled past him and down the marble halls, not running into another soul . . .

Homicide's moniker on the sandblasted pane stared me in the face as I pushed open the door, to the "tack-a-da-tack-a-da-ding" of a lone typewriter under a cloud of cigarette smoke. It was Sid Cranepool, the rookie of the seven detectives under Bingham.

"Little OT, Sid?"

Cranepool looked up from his report, an inch of ash dangling from his Chesterfield. "Tom! Yeah, Homicide never sleeps," he replied stretching, then crushed out his cigarette.

Off Sid's desk I picked up an 8X10 glossy, of an old woman laying spread-eagled across a four-poster bed: clothed, mouth agape, eyes shock-wide, trickles of blood showing from her nose and ears. "What've you got?"

Cranepool lit another Chesterfield. "Insurance case. Old gal was insured up the ying-yang. Her son, this GI with a Dishonorable Discharge, was living with her – real bum. She was taking heart medication – tricky shit – same ingredient as rat poison. Turns out, she OD's on the stuff. Guess who the beneficiary was?"

I played along. *"Not the son."*

"Yup. Next day he files a claim against the insurance company, collects ten grand three months later."

"You got enough to bust this ass wipe?"

"Absolutely. The guy's dirty." Cranepool took a long drag from his cigarette and let it out, nodding toward the Chief's office. "So what's with Bingham? He's been acting weird lately."

"Beats me, that's what I'm here to find out. Better not keep the man waiting." I continued up the gauntlet, the familiar "tack-a-da-tack-a-da-ding" resuming . . . "End that son-of-a-bitch," I echoed.

"Done deal."

*   *   *

It was a game: I never knocked before entering Bingham's office. Sure it teed him off, but he never said anything . . .

The uncomfortable silence was like an impending electrical storm, the same tension you'd feel seeing a cobra slither across the floor of a maternity ward. Bingham stood in the shadows with his back to me, looking out his office window and into the night, his hands stuffed deep in his pockets. At six-foot four, he was one of those guys who made as big an impression with his back to you as when he faced you.

"Shut the door, Tom."

I did. Bingham didn't turn from the window.

"So, where are you and Munson with the Jardine case?"

"What, no *'Gee, Tom, it's sure nice of you to cut your vacation short and take this case for me'?*"

"Okay wise guy, thanks. Happy?"

"There were no prints at the crime scene, least none we could work with. Questioned the landlord and the neighbors and got zip. She's got no priors we can find. I suppose Munson's filled you in on the autopsy results."

"He did. Go on."

"We found five-hundred in cash – large bills – in a purse next to the body, along with a matching withdrawal receipt from Security Mutual. They check out. We also found these . . ."

As I'd done throughout the afternoon, I extracted the photo of Lorraine Jardine and the handbill from my breast pocket, placing them on his desk. Bingham turned slowly from the window and into the light, moving toward them. He'd aged ten years, from the inside out. He bent down, his palms flanking the pieces of paper like a general studying a map. As he took in Lorraine Jardine's portrait, he sighed.

"What's this?" Bingham asked, pointing to the Mamba Club handbill.

"Our only lead so far. Piano player's connected; I believe he's a witness. Problem is, he's a junkie."

"A junkie witness?"

I shrugged. "It's all we've got. We're drying him out at my place so we can question him. Now if you don't mind my asking, what's eating you?"

Bingham gestured to the chair across from his desk.

I sat and lit a cigarette. He sat and shoved back the photo and handbill, like they held plague.

"I'm in a shit-load of trouble, Tom. I need this case closed fast and with discretion. That's why I called you. If the DA gets wind of any of this, I'm finished."

"I'm listening."

"What I'm going to tell you stays in this office . . . Ellen's cancer is back, spreading like wildfire. The last three years of our marriage has been, well, platonic, because of her condition. It's been hell . . . Anyway, through the grapevine I hear about this cute call girl, new in town."

"I'll be damned. Lorraine Jardine?"

Bingham nodded. "Ellen was giving a dinner party the night of the murder . . . My only interest now is my wife, and what this might do to her – "

"And keeping it out of the papers."

"I knew you'd understand."

"What's to understand? So what about Lorraine Jardine?"

"Wait just a God-damned minute!" Bingham stopped mashing the arms of his chair long enough to realize it was a fair question. He lowered his head.

"You loved her?"

"You were married once. Remember the slack I cut you during your divorce? So tell me, I'm hanging here with my nuts in a noose and of the seven detectives under me I ask *you* for a little help. Why?"

"Look around, Ed. I'm the only veteran in this precinct who can still count his toes in the shower without his gut blocking the view."

Chapter 5

I wasn't finished grilling Bingham. I'm in way over my head cause my boss, the Chief of LAPD Homicide, a twenty-three year veteran with a spotless record, was banging a chippy young enough to be his daughter, later to be found murdered. He was facing an accessory-after-the-fact beef, a major conflict of interest, the aiding-and-abetting of a prostitute, not to mention being divorced by his cancer-ridden wife of thirty years once the shit hit the fan. There'd be a public crucifixion, and all for a cute piece of tail. Ed knew anyone connected with him was going down too, and he was looking for me to make the whole thing disappear like Houdini. It stank.

"You still got that single-malt scotch I gave you last Christmas?"

"You know I don't drink" Bingham answered, pulling the untouched bottle of 12-year Glenlivet from a lower drawer and setting it at the middle of his desk.

"You'd better start." I crushed out my cigarette, got up to retrieve two glasses flanking a crystal water pitcher on a silver tray, and sat back down. "Call this a bribe, you've got nothing to lose," I said as I cracked the seal and poured a spritz for Bingham, then a double for myself. I tossed back a slug then looked him square in the face. "How many times did you see Lorraine Jardine before she was murdered?"

"Five. We got together the second Sunday of each month, in Laguna Beach."

"How'd you meet her?"

"Like I said, I heard about this exclusive stable, run by a Madame Dubonnet. She caters to high rollers – city councilmen, attorneys, Water and Power . . ."

"Who tipped you?"

"No names, Tom."

"All right. How was it set up?"

"I dialed a number with an 'oxbow' prefix from the lobby of the Beverly Wilshire, got an answering service. They told me to hang up and wait for a call. I did, and five minutes later this woman calls, a colored woman."

"You ever meet this 'Madame Dubonnet'?"

"Never. She was real clear about that."

"Then how'd you know she was colored?"

Bingham shrugged. "Her voice – she was colored – all business too. I'd better tell you Tom, she's clean under any alias; this broad's a pro. She's got dirt on half the 'who's who' in L.A."

"What'd she ask you?"

"First she sizes me up, personal questions like whether I'm married, got kids, a mortgage, stuff like that. Then she says to state my *'make-and-model,'* when and where I want to meet my *'date,'* what sort of *'party'* I want. After that she gives me the price. Strictly cash."

"What'd you do with the number?"

"Tore it up and flushed it down the toilet, after I heard about Lorraine's murder."

"When was the last time you saw Miss Jardine?"

"A week-and-a-half ago, the Sunday before Ellen's dinner party."

"Any witnesses that can place you at the dinner party?"

"Four, five including Ellen."

"Did Miss Jardine mention other johns, any that had threatened her or were into rough stuff?"

"No. Lorraine never talked about her work – 'the life' she called it, except that she wanted out of it." Bingham was holding up like a champ. Me? I poured another shot of his good scotch. I shoved the handbill back across his desk, pointed to the ballpoint scroll and waited for him to take a closer look. "Does this mean anything?" I asked.

Reaching for the glasses he kept in his breast pocket, Bingham put them on and bent over the paper. A glance was all he needed. He looked up and took off his specs. "Yeah. The last time I contacted Madame Dubonnet she said, 'Oh, so *you're* Lorraine's 'Sugar Man'."

"Okay Ed, this one's real important. You said Lorraine Jardine wanted to retire, so let's assume she was making a break from her pimp. It might've been the reason she was murdered. The last time you saw her, did she give any indication she was frightened and looking to you for a way out?" The blood seemed to leave Bingham's face. I'd hit bone.

"It's all we talked about that night."

"So you set up the Security Mutual account?"

"Yeah, from a private funds of mine. Ellen knew nothing about it."

"What'd you promise Lorraine Jardine?"

Bingham choked . . . "That I'd see to it she'd never have to sell herself again."

*   *   *

I'd logged more miles than most cabbies. On the way back to my place I wondered what I'd tell a grand jury, when this case blew up in Bingham's face and the DA charged me as an accessory for withholding evidence.

Munson seemed to take it all in stride after I'd explained the mess, asking if he could get some shuteye while I took my shift watching Inky. I told him to take my bed and made some coffee in preparation for a long night.

"G'night, Tom."

"Night, Munc." He retreated up the hall and was swallowed by the shadows. I heard the bedroom door close.

Inky still slept like a granite paperweight. Shucking my fedora and coat, I sat at the kitchen table with my coffee and notes, unable to turn off my brain. I lit a cigarette.   *Inky White and Ed Bingham: two bees that didn't belong in Lorraine Jardine's honey jar . . .*

There it was again, that soft "plink-plink-plink" of rainfall. My eyelids were losing the battle, the crook of my arm seeming like the softest pillow in the world.

You're a tough guy, pulled scores of all-night shifts on stakeout.

The rain's lullaby, "plink-plink-plink" melted into the "tick-tick-tick" of my Bulova pressed against my left ear . . .

*   *   *

It was dawn when a terrified scream came from the direction of the sofa, followed by the dull "thud" of something hitting the floor. I shot upright, my left palm in a puddle of drool from where my cheek had been.

"Inky?"

"Where da' hell am I?" a shaky voice answered from the shadows near the sofa.

"My place," I answered, groping for the Venetian blinds.

"Who you?"

I jerked the sash cord, shielding my eyes from the shards of sunrise then turned. Inky looked as gaunt and emaciated as the Auschwitz refugees I'd seen in Movietone newsreels. He was having a hard time standing but could see he was a long way from Lennox.

"Name's Dreyfus, we met yesterday. I'm a detective."

"A detective? What you want with me. You 'sposed to be after the bad guys?"

"I'm giving it my best shot," I lied.

Inky looked down at his socks. "My shoes, where's my shoes?"

I pointed toward the foot of the sofa, to his left. He sat in a huff and nervously began slipping them on and lacing them, caressing heel and sole as if they were the Pope's slippers. "Never touch a man's shoes," he mumbled. Munson appeared from the hall, rubbing his head.

"What's going on?"

Inky looked up and pointed. "Who's he?"

"My partner. Name's Munson."

Munson waved. Inky hadn't a clue about yesterday and looked like a cornered cat. Munson moved past him to the kitchen, to make a fresh pot of coffee.

"If I ain't under arrest then what am I doin' here?" Inky asked.

"When we found you at the rescue mission you were running out of options. The Padre was kicking you out, your mother had already kicked you out, the Mamba Club had fired you, and your band split. The horse, remember?"

Inky went sheepish. "Horse? I don't do dat' shit . . . Ain't nobody's business anyway." Squinting, he sized us up. "Don't act like no cops."

"So we've been told. Look, you're not under arrest, I don't care how you get your kicks, and no one's holding you against your will, but if you don't play ball with us your life won't be worth two dead flies on the street."

"Why's 'dat?"

"Cause you saw something you weren't supposed to," Munson answered, handing Inky a mug of coffee. "Lots of sugar, right?"

As we flanked him Inky tried to follow the volley.

"We're investigating a murder – "

Munson and I caught it: the look of fear, that primal reaction to lightening too close to the cave. Inky knew something, but we still didn't know what or how much. The kid was ripe but needed incentive.

"Even if you weren't a suspect, we wouldn't need heroin as an excuse to drag your sorry ass downtown. I could've done it yesterday. We need your help and you need ours."

"We're all you've got," Munson added.

"Yeah, but you don't know what you're askin'," Inky replied.

"Try us."

Inky got up from the sofa, stumbled to the kitchen table and sat. I followed, sat across from him and waited, lighting two cigarettes, handing him one.

"I mean, what's in it for me if I help y'all?" Inky asked.

"I can get you into protective custody, a place you'll be safe, with the ex-prize fighter John Tucker."

"You jivin' me? 'Iron Man' Tucker, you know him?"

"We go back. Munson and I worked his manslaughter beef . . . I hear he's got a piano he can't play."

Chapter 6

A little ancient history:

In 1938 this Negro middleweight contender, John "Iron Man" Tucker, was approached by the mob to take a dive in the fifth against their Dago favorite, Tony "the Stallion" Santino. The money to fix the bout was more than either fighter would see in ten lifetimes. Pride, however, was in "Iron Man's" corner. In the fifth John threw a right out of nowhere that landed square on "the Stallion's" left temple – John's way of saying to the mob, "Fuck you and the 'horse' you rode in on." Tony Santino went down and never got up. After refusing to tank the fight John took the mob's money and went into hiding, with the DA later issuing a warrant against him for manslaughter. Against a boxer, how funny was that? Word on the street was that Sal Gamboa, L.A.'s mob boss, said he'd "Piss on that nigger's grave." The press had had a field day.

Munson and I had built an ironclad case against Gamboa, with a laundry list of bribes and kickbacks between his syndicate, the I.L.G.W.U. and the Teamsters. He'd had a Teamster killed for refusing a bribe.

The long-and-short of it was this: After a face-to-face with Gamboa, he was to call off the hit on John Tucker and let the fighter keep the money for "the insult done his profession," and, persuade Santino's family to drop the manslaughter charge. In exchange, Munson and I would guarantee there wasn't enough evidence for a conviction. You bet Bingham was pissed, but Munson and I never took any heat cause the Chief had had two grand riding on "the Stallion."

*   *   *

Until the sirens sang for him to fix again Inky was smart enough to see some things needing doing: he stank and he was hungry. After stuffing his clothes in a paper bag, I laid out some clean threads from ten years and twenty pounds ago and headed for the kitchen to make breakfast. Munson stood guard on the fire escape, to make sure our guest didn't checkout via the bathroom window.

Inky finally emerged from the bathroom, looking like an ebony Sinatra. Munson had reentered and sat at the table, attacking his breakfast. I didn't expect much conversation while we ate and wasn't disappointed. Inky pounded-down three eggs, six strips of bacon, a stack of pancakes, two glasses of orange juice, and half the pot of coffee, when I placed the photo of Lorraine Jardine in front of him. He glanced at it, wiped his mouth and stated coolly, "My sister did her."

" – Say what?"

"You were 'bout to ask 'bout the white girl, one with her pretty face run over? Bonita did it."

The kid was shaking my world.

"The two was, y' know, tight . . . S' matter, I'm goin' too fast for ya' all?"

Where the hell had I been? 'That's Bonita, she's no good either,' Mrs. White had warned. Munson and I had violated the first sacred oath of a homicide detective: "Never assume," you know, the "it-makes-an-<u>ass</u>-out-of yo<u>u</u>-and-<u>me</u>" bit. Throughout our entire investigation we'd *assumed* Lorraine Jardine's killer was a man. "What'd you see?" I asked.

"Everythin'. I was livin' in my sister's basement, only they didn't think I was home . . . I'd shot-up when I saw headlights, then heard fightin'. They was fightin' a lot by then – 'salt n' pepper' I calls 'em . . . So I get up to look, and sees Bonita slappin' her roun', callin' her a bitch. That's when Bonita stove-in the girl's head with a tire iron she'd pulled from the trunk . . . and me, too scared – too stoned – to stop it . . ."

Munson had forgotten his breakfast and wrote furiously in his notepad while Inky spilled his guts.

"The girl ain't dead yet, can still see her twitchin' on the driveway. Bonita stands over her like she's ready to whack her again then gets in the car . . . *and backs over her head.* Man, I know my sister's fucked-up, but ain't no way I'm dealin' with dis' shit. So, Bonita stuffs her in the trunk, n' jus fore she drives off, pours gasoline over the girl's brains and lights it. Gettin' rid of evidence, right?"

Munson and I nodded. His hands between his knees, Inky retreated somewhere inside himself, rocking forward-and-back. Slowly, I unfolded the handbill and laid it over the photo, pointing to the scroll, 'Your Sugar Man.'

"What can you tell me about this?"

Inky glanced at it, vacant. "Only I didn't write it. That's Bonita's writin'."

"Then you know you were set up to take the fall for the murder."
"Look 'dat way, don't it Sherlock?"
"Does 'Madame Dubonnet' ring a bell?"
"Ought to, she's my pimpin' sister. Ya' already know."
"Yeah, but I needed to hear it from you."

* * *

As Inky sang the picture got crystal clear: an exclusive call-girl operation providing kink and anonymity to L.A.'s fat cats, run by a queen bee who blackmailed her clientele. Madame Dubonnet's stable was all USDA Prime, young would-be starlets whose open legs was their resume. The understanding amongst the players was simple and Madame Dubonnet held all the aces: if a single card was pulled from the deck the entire house would fall. Her trump was Lorraine Jardine, her gold mine and lover – talk about your "tangled web." A twenty-one-year-old tease, this precocious vixen went AC/DC depending on which way the wind blew. But Hollywood had lost its glamour for Lorraine Jardine. It's when she'd met Ed Bingham, her big protective "daddy," that the "house of cards" began to come down around everyone's ears. The beautiful Miss Jardine had become a liability.

We had to move fast.

"Where does Bonita live? Where's she hang out?"

"Hollywood Hills, house off Mulholland . . . La Presso-Pressa somethin'. It's a private road. She hangs at a club called *Billytus*, on Santa Monica Boulevard, Inky answered.

"The Bilitis Club?"

"Yeah, Bill-I-tus, whatever –"

No one was ready for the knock at my door. It was a weak knock followed by my landlady's voice, its usual sweetness tinged with fear.

"Detective Dreyfus, it's Flora Riddle. Would you come to the door . . . please?"

I motioned for Munson to take Inky up the hall and into the bedroom. "Be right there Mrs. Riddle!" I called, rattling some of the breakfast dishes for effect before heading for the door. There weren't more than five bolts and chains to wrestle with, not excessive for a paranoid cop keeping the world at bay . . .

Sykes's squat, pockmarked face appeared from behind Mrs. Riddle's silver-blue beehive. "Well, if it ain't Bingham's toady," I said. "A little early in the day to be busting old ladies?"

Sykes nervously glanced the length of the corridor. "Invite us in for a drink, Dreyfus."

"I usually don't start my drinking till lunch, but why not."

I backed up with my hands raised, Sykes prodding Mrs. Riddle into the foyer then kicking the door shut with the toe of his right shoe.

"Stand next to me Mrs. Riddle," I said looking past her, square at Sykes. "It's all right, he won't shoot."

Mrs. Riddle obeyed.

His right hand filled with a Smith and Wesson the size of a Howitzer, Sykes motioned with his left, "Let's have the hog leg Dreyfus, slow n' easy, butt first."

I did as I was told, slowly handing him my .38 Special.

"You know why I'm here. Where's the nigger?"

"Had to leave – late for his handsome lessons." I wondered how long I could keep up this level of charm as I watched Sykes slide my equalizer into his left coat pocket.

"Not funny, asshole –"

Sykes's smug puss changed to shock in a heartbeat, as though a proctologist were checking his tonsils the hard way. Munson stepped into the light with his Colt 'Detective Special' in Sykes right ear, pivoting carefully with him, taking the Smith Wesson from his hand. I retrieved my gun from Sykes's coat pocket and we trussed him tighter than a Christmas goose, strapping packing tape over his mouth, leaving him basting in his sweat.

"You guys are good!" Mrs. Riddle applauded. His head erupting from the shadows, Inky surveyed the scene before making his entrance.

"Everything cool?"

We nodded it was safe. Inky looked down at the fat face with the big brown Band-Aid over its mouth, then stepped into the foyer and strutted around Sykes like a bantam cock. "I know you! Motha' fucker kicked me in the balls while I was stoned in the alley back of the Mamba." Inky reared his right leg like he was going to return the favor.

"Whoa," I said, holding him back, really not wanting to. Inky shoved against me once then stepped back, showing me his palms.

"It's cool, I'm cool," Inky said. He shook an index finger at Sykes. "Shoe's on the other foot now, pork chop – kick a man when he's down . . . Good work, good work fellas," he said, nodding smug and satisfied.

"You're not going to leave me here with him?" Mrs. Riddle asked, pointing at Sykes who, by this time, was letting loose muffled obscenities.

"Nah, I've got a real treat for our friend here." I knelt next to Sykes and whispered into a cauliflower ear, "You remember your old pal, Ryan?" Sykes went bug-eyed. "He's coming over to talk old times," I said, slapping a crimson cheek before I stood and headed for the phone.

"Who's Ryan?" Mrs. Riddle asked.

"Sykes's old partner," Munson offered. "At forty-five he puts him back walking the beat cause Ryan wouldn't work the street scores this scum was laying down. Ryan's a true-blue stand-up cop, wife and kids."

"Shit bag," Mrs. Riddle hissed at Sykes.

After touching base with Ryan and John Tucker over the phone, I huddled with Munson. Inky had slumped in my easy chair, his face buried in a Life magazine.

"So?" Munson asked.

"Ryan'll be right over, said he 'wouldn't miss this for the world.' John's glad to put up Inky, he's a fan, hopes Inky'll teach him the piano."

"What makes you think the kid will stay put?"

"You kidding? They worship each other. Inky's not dumb, he knows his sister's double-crossed him, wants him dead so he can't testify. It's perfect."

"What about Bingham?"

"Not good, Ellen's dying. He was called to the hospital last night and hasn't checked in since; I don't expect him to when Sykes doesn't report . . . Ed must've cracked to pull a snafu like this."

Mrs. Riddle cleared her throat. "Excuse me, may I leave now? My bridge group is coming at noon."

"I'm sorry Mrs. Riddle, of course." I put on a smile and gently sandwiched her prune cheeks between my palms. "Before you go: for now, *please*, not a word to anyone about what went on here, not even your bridge group; we'll need a deposition from you later, when this is over. Can I count on you?"

"You can count on me," Mrs. Riddle answered. She side stepped Sykes then half-closed the door behind her, poked her blue-coifed head back in. "Shit box," she hissed at him again.

Spent, Sykes could only moan in resignation.

Inky guffawed from behind the Life magazine. "You ofays are crazy!"

"Listen piano boy, what I said about that deposition goes double for you. Lard ass here didn't crash my gate to make nice."

"More like a lynching," Munson offered.

"Get your stuff and let's go," I said to Inky before returning to Munson. "Wait for Ryan, then meet me at the Bilitis Club on Santa Monica Boulevard."

"Funny name for a club."

"Yeah," I answered as I shoved Inky out the door.

Chapter 7

The Riddle Building's subterranean parking lot was the perfect place for a hit, poorly lit and vacant. I coached Inky from the garage elevator: "Stay put till I signal it's clear. When I do, don't drag your feet."

"*Yeah, yeah,*" Inky scoffed.

Moving quickly, I shuffled between the few cars. I unlocked the passenger door to the Buick, shoved the seat forward then scanned the lot again. Satisfied, I motioned for Inky to hurry. He moved in slow motion, a sign he was tired of being ordered around.

"Get in and stay down."

"What for?"

"Cause you're not popular."

Without breaking I saluted Danny, the Riddle Building's uniformed parking attendant, the midday sun slicing the Buick as I turned onto York, heading east toward the Arroyo Seco Parkway.

"Where we goin'?"

"John Tucker's. What kind of car does Bonita drive?" I asked over my shoulder, reaching for the mike.

"New black Cadillac."

"License plates?"

"Weren't no plates, jus' off the showroom floor."

I pressed the mike's 'transmit' button. "Dreyfus, car fifteen, over."

"... Copy fifteen, what's your location?"

I was in luck. It was Stella. "No location Dispatch, just listen."

"... Come again, fifteen?"

"*No location.* Damn-it Stella, listen . . . over?"

"... Copy fifteen. Go ahead, Tom."

"Need an APB on a Bonita Zuella White, AKA 'Madame Dubonnet.' Description: Negro female; twenty-seven; five-feet nine; one-hundred twenty pounds; black hair; brown eyes; mole on left cheek. Drives a black, unlicensed 1946 Cadillac – probably the only one in L.A. She's a murder suspect; approach with caution. Copy?"

"... Copy fifteen ... Fifteen, got a report from L.A. Fire: Found the burned hulk of a late-model Cadillac this morning, canyon below Mulholland: 'suspected arson, no plates, no witnesses'."

"Right. Has Bingham checked in?"

". . . Negative, Tom."

"Thanks, Stella. Fifteen out." I hung up the mike and braked for a light, a bus in the lane alongside, two nuns waving at me from one of its windows. I smiled and waved back. The nuns shook their heads and gestured frantically, toward the back of the Buick. It's when their faces went from earnest to shock that I turned, to find Inky slumped in the back seat giving the finger with both hands.

"Knock it off!"

Inky holstered his weapons across his stomach and chuckled.

The bus had passed at the green when a chorus of honks kicked me into reality. I punched the accelerator. "Another stunt like that and you'll be wearing your ass for a hat!"

"Cool it shamus man, jus' havin' some fun."

"Yeah, well do it on your own time." That earned me thirty seconds of quiet . . .

"Who dis' Bingham?"

"My boss."

"Why's he want me dead?"

"Cause you witnessed the murder, cause your sister's got the muscle to put him up to it, cause he's married and was banging a whore young enough to be his daughter. He's a good man in a desperate situation – not that you give a shit, and if anyone finds out his life is down the toilet. That's about the size of it."

Alameda Boulevard turns into a mixed neighborhood when you leave Compton. Unlike Bonita White, who'd entered the Anglo-Saxon circle of affluence by making prostitution look legit, John Tucker had gained the token acceptance of working-class whites by refusing to compromise his integrity as a boxer. His neighbors may not invite him over for cocktails, but would brag about their celebrity pugilist at the weekly barbecue.

I parked the Buick in the driveway. Inky stayed in the car, sulking like a kid being sent to an orphanage. So I cuffed him.

John Tucker filled the doorway before my finger hit the buzzer, his broad smile illuminating the drab foyer. "Tom! Git'chor white ass in here," he said. I set down the paper bag with Inky's clothes and we mock-sparred, bobbing and weaving like some fraternal initiation. "Damn, it's good to see you!"

"Good to see you, John." The house was warm, with lingering aromas of vanilla pipe tobacco, Lilac Vegetal, fried bacon . . . and something else. "Jeez, it smells great. What're you cooking?"

"Follow your nose," John said, leading the way to the kitchen.

His living room was filled with boxing memorabilia, but not one photo hinting John had family beyond trainers, cut men, sparring partners, and notable fans both famous and infamous. A Steinway upright piano stood against the wall adjacent to the kitchen.

"Got a soufflé in the oven. C'mon in, but don't bang nothin'. Where's the kid?"

"In the car . . . Cold feet I guess."

"Till he gets a whiff of dis." John chuckled to himself, carefully removing the soufflé. The oven mitts on his massive paws looked ridiculous, especially when you considered those hands once pounded men into hamburger. John was proud of his cooking, a talent he'd discovered since hanging up his gloves.

"Recipe calls for six eggs but I use eight, cause that's how my mama did it. Little hooch?"

"You twisting my arm?"

John poured us a stiff belt of bourbon and we toasted old times. He drained his glass in one slug then said, "Soufflé's gotta' sit for we can dig in. Better get Inky."

"You get him. Here, you'll need these," I said, tossing him the keys to the cuffs. I expected the look I got, but it passed when John remembered I was still a cop. He left, out the kitchen door that led to the driveway.

Inky was slouched in the back seat, smoking with his eyes closed, humming Willie Dixon's, *Spoonful*. It'd been tricky getting the pack of cigarettes and lighter out of his jacket pocket with his hands cuffed, then lighting his smoke. *Same 'ol, white cop workin' on a black man*, he thought to himself –

"You comin' in? Got some good eats," John said, his head framed in the open rear window of Dreyfus's Buick.

The unexpected smiling face scared the shit out of Inky and his lit cigarette fell from his lips. He tried catching it with his cuffed hands but wasn't fast enough and it dropped onto his lap. "Fuck!" he yelled, and started thrashing around on the back seat.

By the time John hauled Inky out the kid's crotch was smoldering. All John could think to do was to keep smacking him hard with an oven mitt till he'd snuffed the fire.

Inky kept shouting, "I'm okay, I'm okay!" and finally yanked himself free from the big man.

The handcuffed kid looked pathetic, staring down at the charred hole in his crotch. John couldn't help it and broke out laughing till he doubled over.

"Ain't funny, man; ain't my pants!"

An elderly white woman carrying a bag of groceries picked-up her pace as she passed, darting back glances at the two lunatics.

"S' matter, you never seen a man's *balls* on fire before?" Inky called after her.

By now John was laughing so hard he was crying. "Here, let's get 'dem cuffs off," he said half-choking, moving toward Inky.

Inky drew back. "Dunno, man. Every time you help me I wind up hurtin' worse." He sized up the smiling giant, when it sunk in . . . "You're 'Iron Man' Tucker," Inky said in awe. He held out his wrists.

John held up the keys to the cuffs. "Dat's me, man-with-da'-key. Where else you think you'd be, son?"

I was about to help myself to a second shot of John's good bourbon when he entered from the living room. "Where's Inky?" I asked.

"Lookin' round. Hungry?"

I checked my watch. Bonita knew running would only draw attention, Munson was either waiting for Ryan or on his way to the Bilitis Club, and Bingham was probably at the hospital waiting for word on his wife. "Sure," I answered, starving –

The boogie piano strain built momentum, like a runaway train. It was *Maple Leaf Rag*, played beyond any eight-to-the-bar stride piano I'd ever heard. The framed 'HOME SWEET HOME' sampler began to rattle against the wall nearest the kitchen table.

"Now that's how Joplin should be played," John declared. "Yeah, we'll be fine."

Chapter 8

I'd told Munson to meet me at the Bilitis Club as soon as Ryan showed up at my place. It was 7:15 when I left John Tucker's, heading north on Alameda. En route it occurred to me that I'd forgotten to tell Munson the Bilitis was a lesbian club. As partners go Munson is one of the best detectives on the force, but in social circles he's a fish out of water. With time on his hands and figuring he'd died and gone to heaven, Munson had saddled-up to the bar next to a dame any man would have sold his own mother to the Apaches for – never mind this dame could exchange a seven-dollar bill in threes.

Compared to the Bilitis the Mamba Club was the Vatican, like ozone you could smell the tension from the sidewalk, Marlene Dietrich's sultry torch songs filtering into the damp night air. Stepping inside the unknown, I ran into a butch the size of a fullback – the bouncer it turns out. I flashed the badge.

Not impressed, the bouncer responded, "Do something about your friend, he's annoying the customers."

"Sure," I said, moving toward the bar. His back to me, Munson was still trying hard to make points with the pretty dame, frustrated he was getting nowhere.

"C'mon honey, get your nose outta the air; it's blocking the light."

I heard the "click" but didn't see the switchblade till its business end gleamed within inches of Munson's throat.

"I'm a dyke, so is every bitch in this bar. Understand, or is it too complicated for you?" said the pretty dame.

Munson pivoted, dumbfounded. I waved. Without another word he put money on the bar for his drinks and slid off his stool. Passing the bouncer on our way out, I said to her, "Step outside." She shouted for "Janice!" to cover for her then complied real nice, muttering "dick" under her breath as we made for the door.

Outside, I described Bonita White then showed her the photo of Lorraine Jardine. "Tell me about them," I said. A two-second glance was all she needed.

"That's Lorraine. All the girls were hot for her, until she shacked up with Bonita. Bonita keeps her on a short leash. Bonita owns the place."

I glanced at Munson, who snickered to himself and took notes.

"When's the last time you saw them together?"

"Bonita was in the other night, just before I ended my shift, but she wasn't with Lorraine. I haven't seen Lorraine in . . . four days now. Say, what's with all the questions?"

"Routine investigation, just checking loose ends." I studied the bouncer, close. "We may need to get in touch with you again, later."

"Swell – It's what I live for."

The bouncer spat and turned in a huff for show, retreating into the Bilitis Club. Munson uncorked that guffaw he'd bottled up as we headed for the parking lot. "My car," I said, and slid into the passenger-side of the Buick.

"Now what?" Munson asked, getting in behind the wheel.

"We wait and watch for the bouncer."

In less than a minute she crept out the back and into the drizzle, wearing a white fur coat that made her look like a polar bear. The bouncer scanned the parking lot, then satisfied, headed for a cream-colored DeSoto.

"Follow her and fall back."

"You telling me how to tail someone?"

"No, but five'll-get-you-ten she leads us to Bonita White."

The headlights cut the night on our serpentine climb through the Hollywood Hills, a full moon trying her damnedest to raise her skirts above the silver clouds. It wasn't Munson's fault we'd lost the DeSoto at a downtown railroad crossing. It didn't matter, cause I believed Inky.

La Presa Drive ended in a cul-de-sac, with a few swanky homes worth no less than five hundred grand apiece sharing the glittering vista. Most of the homes were dimly lit, with two weeks worth of newspapers scattered on the driveways while their globetrotting owners were on vacation. We cut the lights and parked, going ahead on foot. At the end of the cul-de-sac an unnamed gravel road wrapped itself around a hill, just as Inky had said. From a padlocked chain dangled a rusted tin sign with **PRIVATE ROAD** painted in block letters.

"You'll make a fine Lieutenant" I quipped, bowing regally to Munson.

"Lieutenant my ass," Munson said as he stepped over the chain.

That uphill quarter-mile stretch of gravel road was a tough reminder of how long it had been since our days at police academy. Doubled-over and wheezing like a couple of old farts, I tapped Munson's shoulder and pointed.

The full moon had made her debut, highlighting the perfect house for a social outcast. Perched atop the shimmering oasis of Los Angeles, the opulent Moorish love nest was a wart on the nose of high society.

As Munson and I approached the house we could make out the DeSoto in the driveway, its trunk open. Other than a side-porch light that outlined the car, the only artificial light seemed to be coming from a back room inside the house. Anyone passing across the living room would be silhouetted against an arched-picture window at the front. We crouched behind a hedge and waited. It started to drizzle again. After a while two highlighted figures started crisscrossing between the picture window and the DeSoto, dumping armfuls of stuff into its trunk. Three trips later, the 'polar bear' closed the trunk and they went back inside.

"They're making their move."

Framed in the picture window the two figures came together in a long embrace and kiss then passed across the living room in opposite directions. I sent Munson to cover the back while I headed for the front door with Bonita White's arrest warrant.

The porch was dark. Five serious knocks on the door didn't get the results I was after. The curtains to my right moved, the porch light didn't go on, and no one answered the door. I drew my .38 from its shoulder holster. It looked like whatever was going to happen was going to happen the hard way.

"This is the po – "

I choked on the "l-i-c-e" as a running shadow caught the corner of my eye, coming from the side of the house. The shadow turned itself into a woman in a white fur coat as she broke across the illuminated driveway.

"Freeze, police!"

The bouncer slipped on the oil slick on the driveway. A gunshot echoed from the back of the house.

"Freeze!" I repeated. After two feeble attempts to stand the bouncer obeyed, raising her hands. Quickly shifting position behind her, using the bouncer as a shield against a stray bullet coming from the rear of the house, I had a clean angle down the length of the driveway. "Munson!" A seven-second eternity passed. No shot, no footfall, no answer.

The bouncer spat. "Cowardly bastard!"

"Shut-up . . . Munson!"

"Keep your shirt on, I'm coming."

Cuffed and towering, a beautiful colored woman was prodded from the shadows at the rear of the house by my partner. In an ermine coat and stiletto heels, Bonita White nearly eclipsed him.

"The dame tried pulling a gat on me" Munson explained, holding up a small-caliber nickel-plated pistol with pearl grips. "Damn-near crapped my Skivvies."

With little chitchat we herded the pair down the gravel road to the Buick, the whole way I'm thinking: *For two veteran cops, we don't know shit from Shinola.*

The night was far from over.

Chapter 9

John sat, smoking his pipe, half-reading the sports page as he peered over his glasses at his guest. Inky sat noodling at the piano.

"Where'd you learn to play like that?"

Inky turned quickly, like he'd been caught doing what he was really thinking about.

"My mama. Bout' all I ever got from her . . ."

John broke the awkward silence after Inky's reply; being it was his house he wanted to get the ground rules out of the way.

"It's tuggin' at you, ain't it?"

"What you talkin' bout, ol' man?"

"You need a fix."

"I appreciate you puttin' me up n' all, but you're fulla' shit."

"Maybe, but I shot hop fore you was a gleam in your mama's eye – killed a man for tryin' to steal my fix. Kickin' that monkey made me a fighter, son. A champion."

"Yeah, well you're lookin' at the champion of bad luck n' trouble."

Tearing the specs from the bridge of his nose, John led with a jab. "Let me give you some A-B-C advice, boy. You got talent men would die for, and you're pissin'-it away on horse. Any nigger can shoot himself to Palookaville. You best get straight, son, cause you're a long time dead. Then ain't no one gonna remember your name."

Suddenly tired, Inky didn't argue. He needed a fix bad and owed this old Tom no explanation. "Been a long day," he said getting up from the piano bench, "think I'll turn in."

"Wait," John said. "Please?"

Inky stopped on his way to the hall, then turned slowly. "What?" The big man's eyes were pleading, like a whipped dog's.

"Always wanted to learn piano, but ain't had no one to teach me. How 'bout givin' an old man his first lesson? Promise not to needle you no more 'bout the hop," John said with a smile as warm as a bellyful of his soufflé.

"Dunno man, it's late and – "

"C'mon, son. What else you got to do . . . besides?"

"Oh, man." Inky shook his head in resignation and returned to the piano bench. "All right, git'chor lazy gorilla-ass outta the chair."

John obeyed with anticipation like Christmas, sitting down alongside his young mentor.

Inky held out his long fingers at the boxer. "Take a good look at the hands of a piano man," he said. The big man appraised them then nodded he was ready. "Lemme' see yours," Inky ordered.

John held out his callused paws, with their stubby digits.

"Hopeless." Instinctively, Inky placed his fingers at the center of the keyboard. "Look here."

John looked down at Inky's fingers, poised over the Steinway's keys.

"This here's 'middle C'; it's where you start when you wanna' play anything.
Got it?"

John nodded.

Inky drew his hands from the keys. "Show me."

Without hesitation the boxer did, getting the finger placement right his first try.

"Not bad . . . Now play it."

Like a piston, John's fingertips became extensions of his arms and thrust down. The recoil was 'middle C' with the impact of a right hook, the unblemished note resonating throughout the house.

Recovering, Inky reached for his jaw. "Believe you loosened a filling," he said.

"Did good, huh?"

"Oh, yeah." Inky got up from the bench and leaned over the keys. "Gonna' show you somethin' else 'fore I hit the sack. It's called *doe-ray-me*. You learn this and you can play anything only cause you be sick of hearin' it again." Inky moved his fingers through the basic keystrokes he'd learned before walking, watching John's face to see he got it. John nodded he did. Backing away Inky said, "Now practice that – quietly – and I'll show you more tomorrow."

Pivoting on the bench, John watched the young man's eagerness to retreat.

Again, Inky stopped at the entrance to the hallway and turned . . . "Thanks for all you done," he said before disappearing into the shadows.

*   *   *

Feeling he'd hidden the shaking pretty well, Inky lay on the comfortable bed and smoked in the dark, listening to John practice, waiting for the footfall he knew would stop before his bedroom door. Around 1:30 a sliver of light pierced his room from the bottom of the door, then the sound of a door closing from across the hall. Inky could feel the sweat pearling on his forehead as he waited for the big man's snoring, all-the-while tapping the toes of his shoes together with the cadence of a metronome.

Mike McCune

Chapter 10

The drizzle kept up when we got to Lincoln Heights Jail, where women are booked and held for arraignment. The bouncer had started a beef from the back seat, ratting on her partner while denying any involvement in the murder of Lorraine Jardine. "You're dead, bitch" Bonita spit as we ushered her from the Buick. Munson turned to pry the butch from the upholstery.

A half-block away an eight-ton steak bed was barreling a load of bananas in our direction, the driver singing *Noche de Ronda* to the beat of his windshield wipers.

It was the fastest knee to the groin I never saw coming. Her wrists cuffed behind her, Bonita broke across Avenue Nineteen; doubled over I could hear high heels "clicking" and horns "honking." I choked to keep from puking, groped for but couldn't find my .38, heard Munson yell, "Freeze!" In slow motion I stood, saw Munson mouth "J-e-s-u-s," then turned.

It's a sound you hear in your gut: the "dull thud" of rolling steel hitting flesh and bone, followed by the late "screech" of wet breaks. The impact sent Bonita flying over the truck's cab like a broken dervish until she fell in a heap, her shoes pounded off, bananas falling in a nimbus around her. Numb, all that came to mind was Carmen Miranda and *Boom-chicky-boom-chicky-boom*.

Traffic at a standstill, a crowd of rubbernecks converged around the splayed woman, the driver of the truck gesturing as he repeated in broken English, "I deen't see her." Munson and two male pedestrians struggled to restrain the bouncer, who kept crying "Bonita!" into the damp night, while cops spilled from the nearby precinct to deal with the mess. Me? I just stood there, bent over, holding onto my balls.

It took three hailing calls on my frequency before I limped to answer the radio. If anyone could transform dispatch litany into poetry it was Stella.

"... Car fifteen, car fifteen ... 1590 Alameda; man reports his son found dead, over."

My heart sank to the abyss as I thought, *Christ, no.* "Copy, Dispatch ... Need an ambulance to Lincoln Heights Jail, Avenue Nineteen. Also, send a squad car to my place, apartment 203, the Riddle Building on York. They'll find detective Sykes under guard. Book him, charging 'obstruction of justice' and 'attempted kidnapping' of a material witness. You got that, Stella?"

" . . . Sykes?"

"Affirmative. We've got three witnesses to the charges . . . a fourth's dead."

" . . . Tom, we found Chief Bingham in a Laguna Beach motel; looks like a suicide. Ellen died this morning."

"Fifteen out."

I slumped behind the wheel of the Buick with the mike in my lap, crawling somewhere inside myself. Lorraine Jardine's case was closed but there were more jacks to pick up. Munson could handle it from here.

* * *

The law is black or white. As a cop you're trained to accept this, otherwise you go nuts. It's only after you've been around awhile that you discover people are shades of gray, that the law hasn't changed and never will, that maybe you really are nuts.

It wasn't Inky's fault his entire family were no good, that by the time John Tucker entered the picture it was too late for a real father. The kid had been alone his whole life. I've seen first-hand what the mean streets can do to people waiting for an even break . . . Hell, without those mean streets I'd be out of a job.

The door to 1590 Alameda was open. John Tucker was sitting at the Steinway upright with his back to me, hammering *doe-ray-me* over and over on the keys. He ignored me as I passed him and continued up the hall.

Like Lorraine Jardine I found Inky on the bathroom floor, smiling up at me, the hypo still in his arm. He'd finally reached the Kingdom to find the neon "vacancy" sign lit. His left shoe was off and lay next to him, its sole peeled back with urgency, dried blood under the nails of the right hand, the trick heel of the shoe open and hollow. The horse must've kicked his heart like a thunderbolt but it was a peaceful smile, almost smug, frozen now for me to get a long-enough look. It was that rare smile, the kind that reads 'I hold the secret of the universe but I'm not sharing it with you sons-a-bitches,' a smile that would take the coroner three days of steady work to wipe from Inky's face.

Clemens Kalischer

Jake Leg

Mike McCune

Chapter 1

1949 was one of the hottest summers on record in Los Angeles. Add a full moon to the equation and some already-bent people can snap when the heat doesn't let up. That's when L.A.P.D Homicide puts in a lot of OT.

Tuesday, 7:45 am

An hour behind the call, Munson and I elbowed our way past the rubbernecks at a vacant lot on Avalon Boulevard, to where Sergeant Mulcahy held back the crowd. Mulcahy was a veteran cop who'd never made the grade as detective and held a grudge. My having been bumped to Lieutenant didn't improve his attitude.

"Nice of you fellas ta' show up before the stiff explodes."

"Real comedian, Mulcahy. Who found it?"

"Kid over there."

The Sergeant pointed to a colored girl in a pink dress flanked by three cops. The girl looked to be about ten. She was covering her eyes, shaking her head. Crying?

"Let's take the stiff first," I said to Munson, who fiddled with the f/stops on the Speed Graphic while chewing his wad of Beemans. We took turns dipping our fingers into the jar of runny Vicks Vapor Rub I'd pulled from my pocket, smearing a healthy dose under our nostrils. "See you around, Mulcahy."

"Thanks fer'tha warnin'."

As we approached the center of the lot it became obvious why the girl in the pink dress covered her eyes; she'd be having nightmares the rest of her life. Munson spat his wad of gum. "Now there's something you don't see every day," he said.

He was right. Fat flies ricocheted off the bloated corpse of a Negro male who'd been trussed into contortions grotesque and obscene, limbs and head facing directions they shouldn't. Whatever ligatures the killer had used were buried deep into the putrefying flesh. The body had been dumped at the center of the lot without effort to conceal it, and would've been nude except for the argyle socks in scuffed-up loafers that pointed skyward. This guy had died slow: his Achilles tendons slashed and knees broken to prevent him from escaping, fingers and thumbs cut off at the knuckle. He probably didn't say much while all this was going on cause in his toothless mouth was stuffed the appendage meant for pissing from.

A note made from cut-and-pasted newsprint was tied with baby-blue ribbon around the left ankle. It read, **HAPPY EVER AFTER**.

I knelt with Munson alongside the body, cocked back my fedora. "Killer made damn sure we'd spend the rest of the summer ID'ing this." I pointed to the victim's neck. "We got ligature marks here. Looks like they're from a sash cord. Strangulation?"

Munson looked closer and shrugged. "Maybe. Wouldn't have put up much of a fight if he'd passed out, drunk or drugged."

"Anything else?"

"No wallet or personal effects except the socks and shoes. My guess, he's been dead at least a week."

"No way our killer did this here."

"Nah," Munson agreed, "took time and too noisy. Done somewhere private."

Mulcahy had assured us the crime scene was fresh, that no one had touched a thing since police had sealed off the lot. "No sweat about press. Press don't cover shine town," he'd added. Munson was photographing angles of the corpse and I was jotting notes, when county coroner, Cal Colder arrived. "You guys better get what you want off him, he's getting pretty ripe," he said.

"Bag the socks and shoes, then ice him," I answered. It'd take Cal a lot longer to pull evidence from an autopsy than anything Munson and I were hoping to find here. I headed for the girl, figuring my face would be a break from the three cops still circling her like vultures.

"Thanks fellas, I'll take it from here." They looked at me as though I'd robbed their kids' piggy banks. "Don't you wanna know what we got, Lieutenant?" the tallest one asked. "I'll expect your reports soon as I get back to headquarters. Thanks." I eyeballed them hard to make sure they caught my drift. They did and left, mumbling amongst themselves.

I turned to the girl. "Name's Tom. I'm a detective. Sorry you had to see this . . . Really, I am." She turned away and scrunched her shoulders, buried her face deeper into her palms till I thought it would come out the backs of her hands. "My job is to stop bad people. Guess I can't stop them all the time, but I try." . . . That got me squat. "Honey, I can't stop bad people if no one will tell me what they saw." After a ten-second standoff came a muffled reply from behind her palms.

"What you want to know then?"

"Well, you're name would be a start." She turned back, her palms slowly parting to reveal tear-stained cheeks the color of caramel.

"Alice, my name's Alice."

"Okay, Alice. What'd you see?" She pointed to the obvious.

"Dead man, all in a lump over there."

"So you didn't see anyone near the body?"

"Was just there's all. Was on my way to school, was no one with me. Couldn't tell what it was – till I look closer . . . Don't want to talk 'bout it no more."

"Don't blame you . . . One more question, honey, then I'll leave you alone. It's important." She thought about it then gave a half-hearted nod. "On your way to school, was anyone else walking down Avalon Boulevard?"

"None close by. Saw a tall white man, 'bout a block away. He was totin' a red wagon."

"A wagon?"

"You know, a Radio Flyer. Ain't you got kids?"

"No." *Little wisenheimer.* "Did any of the officers call your folks?"

"No, cause they'd be here by now!"

"You're right. I'll call them, and I'll stay till they get here. Okay?" She wiped her cheeks with the heels of her hands and nodded, about the time Munson came over. I shook my head to let him know I'd drawn a blank. "Honey, this is Munson, my partner." Each muttered an uncomfortable, "Hi." "Three of 'L.A.'s finest' and they didn't bother to call her parents. What's your phone number, honey?"

"OXBOW seven-seven-three-nine-four – Stop callin' me *honey*. My name's Alice."

* * *

I put in the call to Alice's folks, who were naturally shook up after the school had phoned to tell them their daughter wasn't there because she'd been 'detained by the police, after discovering the nude body of a murdered man.' It'd been a full day for their little girl.

My baby-sitting duties allowed Cal to finish first. Having bagged the corpse, the coroner and his team were on their way to the morgue for what I hoped would be a fruitful autopsy.

"No point in both of us waiting," I said to Munson. "We need to sweep the lot for any tread-marks or shoe prints, and I want to know who holds title to the property." "Right," he said, and left to round up some of the rookies, Sergeant Mulcahy probably having gone home to bitch to his wife about how I'd bungled the initial investigation.

The parents were less of a problem than I'd expected, more concerned for their daughter's safety than mad at me for the hard questions I'd needed to ask. Handing them my card I let them know how proud they should be of 'such a brave girl,' that I appreciated their cooperation. "Call anytime, I'll get the message." Other than Alice being asked to testify in court, her folks had no stake in any of this. I left them, angry.

Good people and such a sick world; having to trust a wreck like me.

*   *   *

Munson flicked his cigarette out the passenger-side window and stared at the blur of used car lots that flashed by. "Murder for passion or profit, okay. But this psycho shit?"

His remark was so out-of-the-blue that I felt like stopping the Buick in the middle of Figueroa just to hear him repeat it. "Eleven years of partnership and that's the first personal thing I've heard come outta your mouth."

"Ah, skip it."

"Easy, I'm with you. Every time one of these head cases gets loose I feel like retiring myself, till I wise up. And when I wise up I say, 'Dreyfus, it's time to blow this sicko out of his socks before he kills someone else and cops an insanity plea'." Munson glanced at me with eyes that reflect a career of other people's pain. "Right" was all he said, lighting another cigarette and resuming his staring out the window. "By the way, did you find any tire tracks?" I asked.

"Yeah, we found tire tracks. But they weren't from any car or truck."

"Come again?"

"The tracks we found were from little tires, like from one of those wagons kids pull around."

Chapter 2

Stopped at a light not three blocks from City Hall, Stella's dispatch litany sounded over the radio.

" . . . Car fifteen, come in fifteen, over."

I snatched the mike. "Fifteen, dispatch, we read you."

" . . . Report a DB, sixteen-hundred block of Nickerson Gardens, west Slauson, over."

"Ten-four, on our way."

The post-war Nickerson Gardens housing project was everything you'd figure a prison would look like, without the barbed wire and guard towers. Sweating from our toenails, Munson and I shucked our coats and hats, tossing them on the back seat. A big colored guy in denim overalls met us, introducing himself as Spence. After shaking a callused hand big enough to sit in, Spence led us to an enormous avocado tree on the outskirts of the projects. As we approached I counted a dozen people standing beneath the big tree, looking up at something I couldn't make out.

"Wouldn't have noticed a thing," Spence said, "cept' for the smell n' them yellow jackets swarming."

It was the same rendered-fat stink as at the vacant lot on Avalon Boulevard. I looked up, into the guts of the tree. There, from a limb about midway, hung a gunnysack tethered to a yard of rope, yellow jackets swarming frenzied around it. Munson and I looked at one another, each with a pretty good idea what was in that sack.

The people of Nickerson Gardens were used to cops showing up, either to bust a junkie, stop a domestic dispute, or haul away a couple of drunks at the weekly barbecue. This was different.

"Spence?"

"Lieutenant?"

"This could get ugly. I can't conduct an investigation with people milling around, so I'd like your help clearing them away. Might not go over so good if Munson and I do it."

"You bet," Spence said, and turned and walked toward his neighbors. "All right folks, the Lieutenant asks we move along so they can do their job. Guess we done seen everything there is to see, so let 'em be . . . Go on home now."

We watched the twelve disperse, mumbling amongst themselves, and retreat across the hot pavement to their cellblock apartments. Spence followed.

"We need to get on the horn to L.A. Fire, get a unit out here with ladders and bee suits," I said to Munson. "Backup wouldn't be a bad idea, couple of cops to keep gatecrashers away." Munson nodded and left to get Stella on the radio.

I planted my ass in the shade of the avocado tree and lit a cigarette, putting up with the stink rather than fry my brains in the open. Munson joined me, the two of us smoking, moving as little as possible for the next forty-five minutes . . .

* * *

"What's taking so God-damned long? Those yellow jackets are making a smorgasbord of the evidence."

"Fire call. We're in the middle of a draught, remember?"

Spent and amazed, Munson and I watched the wavy giant in denim overalls, as he crossed the shimmering pavement toward us. We noticed he carried a glass pitcher with the "clinking" sound of ice in it.

Spence smiled and shook his head at the pathetic sight: two middle-aged detectives in shirtsleeves and loosened ties, reclining in the dirt under a tree, sweating, waiting. Setting down the pitcher and two glasses he said, "Wife figured some lemonade might go good about now."

"Spence, you're a hero," I said, pouring a glass full and handing it to Munson. "Man, that hits the spot," he managed between gulps. I poured a glass for myself and savored the cool, tart-sweet liquid as it bathed my parched throat.

"Nothin' like lemonade to cut the tar on a day like this," Spence said. "No luck with the Fire Department?"

I wiped my mouth with the back of my wrist. "They'll be here."

"More lemonade?"

"Nah, we're good, thanks." Spence bent to collect his empty pitcher and glasses. We locked eyes for an instant. "Thank your wife for us," I said. "You bet," he answered, before walking away into the bleached pavement, the mirage swallowing him for the last time . . .

* * *

I was working on my fifth cigarette, humming Nat Cole's *Mona Lisa*, when the big red fire truck pulled up with its blinding chrome. I shielded my eyes and squinted. It was a lean, tired face, streaked with sweat and soot that asked, "What've you got, Lieutenant?" If that face wasn't twenty years younger I would've felt pretty shitty about bothering him. I pointed up. "That gunnysack with the yellow jackets around it? Need it down – gently."

Following my finger lean-face shrugged, "It's your nickel." He gestured at the truck. "Johnny, we'll need the extension ladder and a smoke pot!"

"You squeamish?" I asked. Lean-face studied me as he climbed into his bee suit, put on its headgear with its mesh face-guard.

"Lieutenant, I just pulled three charred bodies from a warehouse, their blood still boiling. I pulled and their skin came off the bone. I'm sure I can handle whatever's in the sack."

Lean-face let out the extension ladder, nestling its U-shaped end against the thick trunk, just beneath the gunnysack. Johnny squatted and set the smoke pot at the base of the avocado tree.

"What'll that do?" I asked.

"Smoke pot? It's like a tranquilizer to most insects; they get a dose and they drop like rain. Yellow jackets? Tough little bastards, meat eaters – It'll probably tick 'em off."

Word of 'a dead baby in the gunnysack' had spread throughout Nickerson Gardens and, despite the one-hundred-and-five degree heat, most of the residents now congregated from across the shimmering pavement to watch the show. I felt better when a squad car pulled up and cops began to cordon off the crime scene.

Johnny lit the smoke pot. Well away from the avocado tree, Munson, lean-face and I watched, as billowing smoke engulfed the gunnysack. When the smoke finally cleared most of the yellow jackets lay scattered in the dirt at the base of the tree. His head gear on, lean-face scrambled up the ladder.

" . . . There's a note! It's attached with pink ribbon!"

I cupped my hands over my mouth. "What's it say?" Lean-face stretched out a gloved hand, grabbing for the rope.

"Shit – Heads-up!"

Munson and I backed away in time, just as the gunnysack hit

the ground with a "plop." A viscous fluid wept from the burlap, its stench overwhelming.

"Sorry!" called lean-face, and scrambled back down the ladder.

I went for the pink ribbon and note: the same cut-and-pasted-newsprint type as on the Avalon body. Munson leaned over my shoulder, the firemen joining him. "What's it say?" he mumbled through his handkerchief.

I walked away without answering, to the Buick to get a morgue bag.

"'*To get ahead, one needs a hand.*' What's that supposed to mean?" Munson called after me.

"Beats the hell out of me!"

Chapter 3

With bemused detachment Cal Colder set the gunnysack on the stainless steel table, three dead yellow jackets still clinging. Using surgical scissors the coroner freed the pink ribbon and its note, handing them to me. He cut the sash cord that cinched the opening then peered inside without so much as a burp. "Well, I can tell you what it isn't," he said. "It's not a fetus." Grabbing the base of the sack with both gloved hands he lifted, the milky contents sluggishly rolling out onto the coroner's table.

"Then what-the-fuck is it?" Munson asked in disgust.

"A haggis," Colder replied, "the stomach of a goat with something sewn inside." He pointed at stitches running the length of the blue-veined, pasty-gray organ, about the size and shape of a football. I pocketed the note and lit a cigarette, Cal turning to me.

"Please, Lieutenant, I've asked you not to smoke in here."

"Sorry." Looking around, I dropped my cigarette into the trough of water running the length of the coroner's table, watching till it disappeared down the drain. Cal shook his head and returned to the goat stomach. Taking his surgical scissors, he carefully began cutting the sutures till a cavity opened, the rest of the foul-smelling fluid spilling out along with stuff that looked like Quaker Oats.

It was like watching an obstetrician deliver a midget's baby: Cal thrust a hand into the bladder, raising his eyes questioningly a couple of times. There was a "sucking" sound as he slowly extracted . . . "A woman's left hand," he announced.

Like the male victim, the fingers and thumb had been cut off at the knuckle. I pulled the latest note from my breast pocket and held it out. "'To get *ahead*, one needs *a hand.*' Our man's talking in riddles . . . Cal, did you autopsy the Avalon body?"

"Yes. Strangulation was the cause of death. Breakage and contortion of the limbs and neck, along with the victim's severed penis, were all postmortem . . . There was evidence of molestation, also postmortem."

"Great, he's a frickin' pervert, too" Munson offered.

"Would seem so," Colder replied. "Getting an exact measurement from a decaying and trussed corpse wasn't easy, but the victim was about five-foot ten-and-a-half. I place the age anywhere from thirty-five to forty-five. All means of identifying him are missing, so he's definitely a 'John Doe.' And, since we're into stomach contents – those I could find after such decomposition – residual traces of grain alcohol usually dissipate in heat, but the victim was saturated with the stuff, enough to paralyze him. It's called 'jake leg.' This might explain why there are no signs of him resisting his killer – "

We turned at the knock on the door as a member of Colder's staff entered, a young pimply-faced kid in a white coat.

"Lieutenant, there's a call for you."

I pointed to the phone on Colder's desk. "Go ahead," he said, removing his surgical gloves.

"Dreyfus . . . What? You sure? Son of a bitch!" I slammed down the phone.

"What?" Munson asked, shrugging.

"While we've been poking at goat guts our man's been back to the lot. Someone found another gunnysack. This one's got a woman's head in it: to 'get *a head* one needs a *hand*.' He's been watching us the whole time."

Detectives working cold-case files too long can go soft and lose their edge. It's a sad fact, when you get a real case, one you can sink your teeth into, you're almost grateful. Two victims and we had an MO. Okay, our killer was a sicko, but he was bright and wanted to play. Well so did we, opposing egos playing a big part here. The long-and-short of it was this: beat as tambourines, Munson and I returned to the lot on Avalon Boulevard, put up with more of Mulcahy's griping, photographed and bagged the gunnysack with the head in it, combed the lot and found more tire tracks from a wagon. What we weren't prepared for was the bum standing at the end of the lot yelling, "Go team, go!"

I gave this goof the 'come-hither' finger. He pointed at his chest and played dumb. Before the bum could make a break, Mulcahy put a big paw on his shoulder and shoved him forward.

"All right, Mac, don't be shy. The Lieutenant would like a word with 'ya."

It was a burnt, shoe-leather face with rheumy eyes set in dark sockets. The guy's BO was enough to drop a stampeding water buffalo. "What's the rush?" I asked, watching those rheumy eyes twitch. "I know you're just itching to tell me something."

"Like what?"

Mulcahy's fingers chewed the bum's shoulder.

"Hey, that hurts!"

"Then sing, Mac," said Mulcahy.

Munson had his pencil and notepad ready.

"The gunnysack; any idea who put it there?" I asked.

"How-the-hell should I know?"

Mulcahy kneaded the shoulder again, till the bum listed and buckled.

"All right, all right. I saw a tall guy wearin' a khaki cap and GI coat. He was pullin' a red wagon."

I glanced at Munson. "You see this guy put the gunnysack in the middle of the lot?"

"Nah. He was walkin' away, about a half-block or so."

"Which direction?" With his free arm the bum pointed northeast, same as the colored girl had this morning.

"So what's with the pep-squad routine?" Munson asked.

The bum looked over his shoulder at Mulcahy, then down at the big hand that was mashing it. I nodded and Mulcahy let go. The bum rotated the shoulder repeatedly, not sure he'd get any feeling there again.

"Some people say I'm a bubble off plumb – you'd be too if you were a gunner in a Sherman. I get this ringin' in my ears that drives me nuts; guess I do some crazy shit. Didn't mean nothin' by it."

"Ever see the tall guy with the wagon before?"

"Sure, lots of times, at the rescue mission. He works for the padre there, runnin' errands n' stuff. He's a shell-shocked vet, too. You think I'm gone? That schmuck is dumber than a sack full of hammers."

"This guy got a name?"

The bum shrugged. "Wouldn't know, he's a mute . . . Say, any you cops got a smoke? I'm dyin' for a cigarette here."

"Absolutely not, Lieutenant, there must be a mistake. Simon's incapable of harming anyone," Father Noonan said.

I remembered him from forty-six, when I'd found Inky White boarding at his Sally Ann, and he remembered me. We'd didn't like each other then, even less now.

"This isn't an indictment, padre, just an investigation. We're trying to keep a killer from killing again, and that means following any leads we get. Two witnesses place a tall guy in Army fatigues pulling a red wagon northeast from the crime scene. That's toward your rescue mission. Now are you going to let me talk to this Simon or do I need a warrant?"

"You can't talk to him, unless you know sign language."

"Can he read?"

"Yes."

"Then get him."

The padre led Simon into the office, each with an attitude as thick as a wooden Indian. Simon sat like a trained monkey. The two started their sign lingo, the padre, I guess, telling him who we are and why we were there. Not a twitch from Simon; as far as he was concerned Munson and I weren't even in the room. Munson got out his notepad and pencil. I did the same and scribbled the question: 'Were you pulling a red wagon near a vacant lot on Avalon Boulevard this morning?' Before shoving my notepad across the desk, I showed my partner what I'd written.

I may as well have been interrogating a suspect with his attorney alongside: The padre picks up the notepad, reads the question and shows it to Simon who, looking up for the first time since entering the room, nods before shoving the notepad back.

Furiously, I scribbled my next question: 'What was in the wagon?' thinking, *This Q & A will take all summer.* Expecting the same Mutt-and-Jeff drill, I hand the notepad to the padre; only this time Simon takes it, reads it, then writes and hands me his answer: '**FOOD**.' The padre must've read my face.

"Every morning at seven o'clock Simon goes to Langer's Grocery to get provisions for the mission – coffee, potatoes, sugar and other staples. These are bulk groceries, packaged in burlap sacks."

Munson and I glanced at each other, feeling like two drunks who'd stumbled into a women's lavatory.

The padre stood slowly and offered a hand, his mute ape following. "When you stop by Langer's say 'hello' for us," he said with a shit-eating grin. I felt like slapping that grin to the back of his head.

Chapter 4

The swamp cooler on full blast, I lay on the davenport with a half-eaten gin and tonic resting comfortably on my stomach. Munson was in the kitchen, frying up a couple of grilled cheese sandwiches. That we'd made it up to my place without my nosy landlady, Mrs. Riddle, engaging us in chitchat was a first, the both of us soaking up silence till the phone rang. I let it ring five times before answering.

"Dreyfus . . . You sure? Thanks, Cal."

"He got us a match on the hand and head?" Munson asked from the kitchen.

"Yup, same blood type. She's still a 'Jane Doe'."

"Them coroners do half our work."

"Ain't it the truth –" The phone rang again. I played smart-ass. "Yung Fuk Laundry, no starchy in Skivvies . . . You're kidding. Where?"

Munson came out from the kitchen, chewing his grilled cheese. The look on his mug said he knew what the call meant.

"Thanks Stella," I said and cradled the phone, looking up. "Another pork. This one is off east Pico."

*   *   *

Two cops pointed halfway down the alley, to where five huge rats were throwing themselves against a trashcan at the back of a Chinese restaurant. "Never seen anything like it," they mumbled. Neither had I.

A Chink in a tux appeared at an alley exit, pinching his nose and pointing at the trashcan. "Mad rlats, mad rlats. Bad fo' business," he repeated before going back inside, slamming the door.

The rats ignored me as I moved closer, drawing my .38 Special and taking aim. The "pop" echoed off the alley walls, one of the rodents exploding fur and blood only to be dragged off by the others. Guess they figured he was an easier meal than the one they were bashing themselves to get at. The two cops were impressed.

"Nice shooting, Lieutenant."

I holstered my gun, turned to Munson and drew a fifty-cent piece from a pocket. "Flip for who opens the lid?"

"Call it," Munson said.

Flipping the coin I called, "Tails," and caught it . . . "Heads."

The stink was overwhelming, a black cloud of flies hovering around the trashcan. Tied to the handle I saw the familiar baby-blue ribbon with another cryptic note and moved closer. The note read: **IT'S A WONDERFUL LIFE**. Covering my mouth with my handkerchief, I reached for the lid, lifting the handle quickly and peering inside. I slammed the lid back down. Retreating past Munson and the two cops I belched, "Torso in chop suey."

*   *   *

Andrew Whitelaw was the epitome of the well-groomed DA: Harvard, vodka martinis, a favorite son of old Los Angeles money, and no stranger to greasing a palm or two on his way to a mayoral candidacy. The cost of his tailor-made silk suit could feed a family of three for a year.

South-central Los Angeles was way off Whitelaw's beat, and the news we brought, that a psychopath was on the loose there was greeted with indifference. The DA was used to tidy domestic murders; as far as he was concerned Chinatown or Compton may as well be on Mars. "Three?" Whitelaw asked, turning an 8X10 glossy (a close-up of the Avalon victim) at every angle and back.

"So far." I leaned across his desk and trued the photo for him. Raising his eyebrows, he set it back down on the pile.

"You've reason to believe there'll be more?"

"Every reason. He enjoys killing," I answered.

"And the coroner confirms each victim was murdered by the same man?"

"Yes."

"Details, please."

"He keeps his victims, sometimes days before dumping them; Cal doesn't believe they were found in the order they were killed. He mutilates them, after they're dead. He's careful about leaving evidence, removing the fingers, thumbs, and teeth. With the second victim, a woman, he left a severed hand. Her head was found later, at the same location as the first victim. Third is a male torso."

"So, as yet, each of the victims is unidentified?"

"That's right. But we've reason to believe they were derelicts." Whitelaw looked at me like he'd never heard the word before.

"Derelicts? How did the two of you arrive at this conclusion?"

"Cal found grain alcohol in each of them. Might suggest they knew their killer," Munson answered.

"I don't see their drinking grain alcohol suggests anything but a hunch."

Sick of the bullshit, I locked eyes with the DA. "I don't know anyone in Brentwood who drinks Everclear, do you?"

"Touche, Lieutenant." Whitelaw opened our report for the first time, slowly moving an index finger down each item.

"The killer leaves notes?"

"Made from cut-and-pasted newsprint. He attaches them to his victims with these." I held out the ribbons. "Blue, a man; pink, a woman. We've dusted everything. No prints."

"Which means, you haven't got a suspect. Why did you come to me with this?"

"To let you know there's a lunatic on the loose who's going to keep on killing till he's caught. He's getting careless." Whitelaw scooped-up the report and photos, tamping them on his desk till he was satisfied they were in line. He handed them back.

"By all means, Lieutenant, catch him. And while you're at it, bring me enough evidence for a conviction."

Mike McCune

Chapter 5

The conversation of two men echoed off the cool concrete vaults of the labarinyth, but if anyone were listening it would have been impossible to tell from which tributary the voices came. But the two men were alone, as damp and cavernous alone as the bowels of a coalmine.

"Care for a refill on your sangria, Mr. Boyle?" said Cole, hoisting a demijohn, three-quarters empty.

"Sangria my ass, you've spiked this Dago red."

"My own vintage."

"Vintage – Cole, you're a hoot!" Boyle bellowed. He thrust his filmy glass at the shadows, where the eyes of his host glowed like smoldering embers. "Great digs this place, you'd never know there's a heat wave goin' on outside." Boyle got his refill.

"I admire your stamina, Mr. Boyle. Most of my guests would have passed out by now," said Cole when he'd finished pouring.

"Ah, the stuff don't know what hit it." Boyle raised his glass in a toast. "I say we make a dead soldier outta your jug," he slurred.

"Excellent idea, Mr. Boyle. To your health," *or what remains of it*.

*   *   *

"Will you look at this pile of crap," Munson said, slapping shut a file, one of seven. "Wives doing husbands, husbands doing wives, and they all got fat insurance policies."

"Ah, the institution of marriage: prostitution and extortion with the State's blessing," I said from the back of my *Los Angeles Times*. Checking yesterday's Hollywood Park results I discovered I'd missed an exacta in the sixth race.

"What're we gonna do with them?"

I peered over the sports page at my partner. "Do? Nothing. We've got our case."

"Chief Parker says we got to give equal time to every case."

"Screw him."

"You won't have to," a voice responded.

The voice was Sid Cranepool's, rookie of seven detectives. Again I peered from behind my paperwork, in the direction of an

Olivetti Underwood's "rat'ta-tat-tat" under curling smoke from a Chesterfield.

"Sid?"

"I'll take your load. Matrimonial and insurance scams are my specialty."

"You sure?"

"Yeah. But I want a promise."

"Name it."

"End the psycho."

Munson and I nodded a duet of assurance at Cranepool, when the phone rang. Munson snatched it, readying his pencil and notepad.

"Homicide, Munson."

" . . . This is Father Noonan, at the rescue mission. We spoke yesterday afternoon."

"Yeah, padre!"

I dropped the sports page.

" . . . I may have information concerning those murders. Can you come down?"

"We're on our way." Munson cradled the phone. "Says he's got a lead. Sounds pretty shook up, and drunk."

The padre gestured and Munson and I took the same seats. His desk seemed to have gained more clutter since yesterday, or maybe it was the empty bottle of Amontillado sherry he was trying to hide behind stacks of files. The padre sat awkwardly and picked up last night's edition of the *Herald Examiner*, opened to page two and the blurb: **TRASHCAN TORSO – Police Baffled By Third Gruesome Find**.

"Before I begin," said the padre, "I must know. You visited Langer's Grocery after leaving here, they confirmed what I told you about Simon's duties at the mission?"

"Don't worry, padre, he's not a suspect. Now why'd you call us?"

"After you left I began thinking, about those murders. Am I to understand you found a third victim?"

"Yes," I answered. The padre let go of the paper and stared past me, vacant, his eyes swollen from too much sherry, too little sleep, and something tearing at him from the inside out.

"I've reason to believe the victims were regulars at our mission," said Father Noonan.

He slid his chair back and reached for a side drawer, extracting two scrapbooks that he placed at the center of his desk.

"I keep a journal of each guest, their comings-and-goings, their past, their progress – or lack of it. It helps to reestablish their identity. You see, addicts feel isolated from society, either because they choose to out of denial, or because society shuns them. They're much like the lepers from Biblical times. Most of those who come here for help were born to the streets. The victims were different."

"How do you mean?" I watched the padre take the first scrapbook and flip to a dog-eared entry that held a couple of photos, some notations and a heading, then turn it around till it faced Munson and me. He pointed to the entry and sighed.

"Joshua Tanner, forty-two, a decorated veteran, married and a father of three. He was one of the original Tuskegee Airmen, and taught English at South Central High School after the war. In 1947 he was brought before the School Board and, after a lengthy and humiliating inquiry, admitted to having sexual relations with one of his female students, a known tease. The resulting scandal cost him his job and his marriage. Joshua took to the streets, becoming an alcoholic."

I studied the photos of a bearded and tired-looking Negro, handsome but the face puffy and old before his time. There was no way to confirm him as the Avalon body. "I'm sorry padre, but this isn't–" Then I caught it: In both photos the man was wearing pants that were too short, displaying argyle socks and loafers. Munson caught it too.

"There's more," Father Noonan said. Taking the scrapbook, he flipped rapidly to another mangled entry. Again, he turned the scrapbook around and held it out.

I took it. Under the heading 'Lillian Cavanaugh' were a series of dates and notations, and three photos of a woman who cornered the market on ugly. The woman in the photos wore a butch haircut, and a permanent scowl that seemed to suggest she held a beef with the world in general.

"Lillian came to the mission shortly after Mr. Tanner. She was head nurse in the maternity wing of Glendale Memorial Hospital. Los Angeles saw a record number of births in nineteen forty-eight, obstetricians and nurses working exhausting overtime to keep pace. Miss Cavanaugh had been working fourteen-hour shifts. On the evening of October third she'd slipped out of the nursery, to get a sandwich. She was gone only five minutes, but when she returned one of the infants had turned in its bassinet and suffocated. 'Crib death' it's called. Lillian tried repeatedly to revive the baby, but it was no use. That child was the only son of Baxter and Emma Hollingsworth."

"Standard Oil?" Munson asked. The padre nodded then seemed to drift into a trance.

" . . . When they were here they kept to themselves, a private circle no one else was allowed to enter."

"Come again?" I asked.

"Joshua, Lillian, and the others," Father Noonan answered, flipping to several marked entries in the second volume before presenting it to me. "Like I told you, Lieutenant, they were once respected members of society, but each had a fall from grace. That's why they felt safe around one another, they understood how fickle life can be."

The padre pointed to a photo, of a tall man seated at the head of a cafeteria table with five others seated around him: three men, two women. The five included Tanner and Cavanaugh. Bums, yet all of them were laughing as though they'd won the Irish Sweepstakes.

"That's John Cole – 'King' Cole they called him, one of the most brilliant yet troubled men I've ever met. A Jeckyll-and-Hyde personality if ever there was one."

"How does he fit in?"

"I don't know that he does, but it's been three months since I've seen John Cole or the others. Sure, they'd relapse; go off on a bender for a week or two then return. But while they were here Cole kept his disciples sober, and they kept to themselves. He was their anchor, not me – certainly not God. He told them God had abandoned them. How could I argue with that, Lieutenant?"

Chapter 6

'Whistle while you work' . . .

He whistled the ditty as he dragged yet another pilgrim by its ankles the length of the aqueduct, studying the face as its head bounced on the damp gravel. It was tiresome work but had to be done. The tune somehow eased the burden.

Boyle was a big man, harder to kill than the others. He'd come to, groping frantically for the sash cord. Even with his throat cut he'd continued to fight. Severing the spinal chord at the base of the lumbar spine had been the answer. Yes, a special trophy from this pilgrim was in order. "Hum, 'Whistle while you work'." Tugging, Cole sighed, "Disney, such genius . . ."

Cole pondered: *And how kind of Mister Mulholland, to provide living quarters with such privacy.* "What was it the man had said? Oh yes, 'There it is. Take it'."

Access to the gates that diverted flash floods from his subterranean kingdom had been easy enough to secure, and a new padlock was all that was required to assure the occasional Water and Power inspector of the status quo. It amused Cole, how farmers of the Owens Valley must have puzzled over the modest rebate of their stolen water.

*   *   *

He poured the body onto the concrete altar, traffic drumming from the street overhead. Rifling the man's pockets didn't take long, a tattered wallet yielding only a five-dollar bill, an expired union card, and a yellowed press clipping.

"Jake Boyle: stevedore, labor leader. Let's see, indictment and union expulsion for receiving kickbacks? You should have been more careful, Mr. Boyle."

Cole looked up at his dangling trophies, each severed head or limb representing another martyr on the compost heap of life. "Such an awesome responsibility. One day you'll thank me for taking away your pain, but first a trip to the medicine cabinet. Doctor must have steady hands if he's to heal the sick."

Finding a vein that hadn't collapsed was getting tricky, but he did and slapped his right calf. The opiate on its way, Cole slumped in a corner, waiting till it took hold, fixing on the gaping cut across

Boyle's throat. He closed his eyes and drifted back into a diaphanous dream, into the mouth of madness . . .

The orderlies bring them in too fast; the oil-smeared burned and maimed, one sailor with ten centimeters of shrapnel protruding from his chest, all screaming in agony.

"Fire on the fore deck! Bridge's exploded! Captain n' the officers – they all went up!" "She's breakin' apart, lads! Abandon ship!" Chaos everywhere and still the orderlies bring more shattered sailors. I administer morphine, apply tourniquets, and placate them. Choking smoke pours into the infirmary. Reagent lists violently. "Leave 'em Cole, they're done for!" my orderlies call before abandoning me. "Get back here you bastards!"

The morphine does no good, the sailors only screaming louder in their delirium. It's a madhouse. I cover my ears with my palms and press. "Shut up, all of you!" Another explosion, and the bulkheads groan their death-knell.

The Reagent lists again as I grope my way to the pharmaceuticals, choking "I'll find the strength to do what I must." Clenching the rubber surgical tube in my teeth, the vein bulges and I plunge the hypodermic home. The narcotic rushes as I crawl to my desk, reaching feebly for the drawer holding the Webley. Everything becomes clear as I load the revolver. I turn to the injured sailors who look up at me, pleading.

I am God. "Doctor will see you now."

Chapter 7

Cal confirmed, the torso found in the alley off east Pico was a male's, its genitalia intact. The victim's back and buttocks, however, displayed something new to the killer's MO: postmortem cigarette burns. No sooner had I finished typing my report when Munson hung up the phone after a twenty-minute call to New York.

"Immigration and Naturalization says five thousand thirty-eight Limeys entered the U.S. between '45 and '48. Forty-two registered under the name of 'Cole;' eighteen were single males in their late thirties to early forties."

"Any register their destination?" Munson handed me his notes . . . "Thirty-five said Los Angeles, and you got their last-known address? You're beautiful!"

"I'm a big detective. I can dress myself and everything."

"Okay wise guy, get your hat. We've got a lot of ground to cover."

As Munson drove to our first stop, an antique shop on Santa Monica Boulevard, I had time to reflect. Cynicism aside, in my fifteen years as a cop I'd prided myself as a pretty good judge of character. But with the padre I'd been way off base. Since our first meeting I'd made up my mind I didn't like the guy, and damned if I knew why. Maybe because he had faith, something I'd given up on long ago. Now, armed with photos of a probable suspect and his victims, which the padre had offered without subpoena, we had our first solid lead. He seemed sure this John Cole was our man and, right now, that was fine with me.

"Okay, we've got three victims, two we've ID'd. That leaves two more Cole wants dead for whatever fucked-up reason. They're all drunks, so he spikes their Thunderbird with Everclear, strangles them after they've passed out, then filets them. He wants us to think he's a pervert. He's cocky, leaves sick notes at the crime scene and makes no effort to hide what he's done. He's on foot, hauling his kills in gunnysacks in a red wagon, and, he's tried pinning the whole thing on a mute vet who works for the padre. Witnesses, zip. I forget anything?"

"Didn't the padre say they were once respectable types that had ran into bad luck? 'Fall from grace' he called it."

"Yeah, so?"

"So, they understand each other. That's how he gets close enough to kill them. And what if Cole had a 'fall from grace' himself, one so bad it drove him over the edge."

"What're you saying?"

"Their lives are so screwed up, maybe this psycho thinks he's doing them a favor by killing them." Munson checked the side-view mirror and announced, "We're here."

*   *   *

The lavender double doors were hard enough on the eyes, but it was the chartreuse cherubs that stood out in relief like Rocky Marciano in lace trunks. The brass doorplate read: *House of Cole*. I turned to Munson.

"You sure this is the place?"

Munson checked at his notes and shrugged.

I looked around for a doorbell; instead pulling a gold cord that rang chimes. After three tugs on the gold cord a slender guy in a caftan answered, with a sad look on his face like maybe he'd broken a fingernail.

"Mr. Cole?"

"Have you ever had a soufflé collapse on the eve of a dinner party?" the guy asked.

"Not lately."

"I suppose there's no point in crying over it. What are you selling?"

"We're not selling anything. I'm Lieutenant Dreyfus and this is detective Munson." I showed him the badge. The guy raised his hands.

"I have my Green Card. I'll get it."

As he turned to retreat from the sunlit foyer I instinctively called, "Hold it!" The guy froze, shaking head-to-toe.

"Better ease up or you'll give him a heart attack," Munson whispered.

"Relax Mr. Cole, we've made a mistake. You're not the man we're looking for."

"I'm not?"

He sounded disappointed, his arms falling to his sides. "Sorry to bother you," I said and turned to leave.

"Lieutenant? If you've a photo of him, I'd like to see it."

I stopped, pivoted, the guy giving me a soft smile and a shrug.

"Just curious. I'd like to see the 'Mister Cole' I'm supposed to be."

Extracting the photo from my shirt pocket, I held it out. The guy's face read boxcars.

"I know this man, from Ellis Island! Fascinating chap, only he didn't give his name as 'Cole,' simply used the initials 'J.C.' – You can imagine my surprise, we're both from Sussex."

Munson scribbled furiously on his notepad.

"Fine. So you talked?"

"Well, yes. He said he'd served as a ship's surgeon during the war. Royal Navy, of course."

"Thanks for clearing that up. Did he mention the ship he served on?" The guy tucked one hand under an armpit and gingerly stroked his chin with the other.

"Dear . . . Yes, the *Reagent*, that's it, H.M.S. Reagent, a cruiser I believe . . . Tragic."

"How?"

"*Reagent* took two torpedoes in the North Atlantic, caught fire and broke apart before sinking. Half her crew went down, including all the officers but J.C. Oh, the lives that poor man tried to save. A miracle he survived the ordeal."

"Has he been in touch since?" The question seemed to bring the guy back from somewhere far off and he dismissed it with a wave.

"Goodness no, that was the last I saw of him – pity, such a handsome chap, and so tall. Now, if that is all detectives, I must prepare for guests, buyers from Berlin looking for a steal on Tiffany lamps."

Munson slid behind the wheel and mopped his brow. I slouched on the passenger seat, alongside. "Will this heat ever let up?"

"Ninety-seven," Munson said, tapping the thermometer we'd had mounted on the dashboard.

"What's our next stop?"

"El Segundo."

"El Segundo? Too far from the killings, our man's on foot. Anything within the radius?"

Munson checked the map and shook his head. "Nothing. Got a 'Cole' showing as far north as Oxnard, another as far south as Escondido – "

". . . Car fifteen, 'dispatch' fifteen."

"You get it."

Munson took the mike. "Fifteen, 'dispatch,' we read you."

". . . DB call: Hollywood High football field, over."

Munson shrugged.

"Give me that," I said, taking the mike from Munson. "Come again, Stella?"

". . . A 'dead body;' this one's hanging from a goal post. Over."

"You heard the woman, let's go."

Hollywood High was deserted, its summer sports programs canceled because of the heat wave and budget cuts. The fields of the campus were brown, the brick dust of the track and baseball diamond dry as a teetotalling spinster, an occasional zephyr whipping up little red clouds with a bubblegum wrapper or two.

The janitor had found it. "Hardly go out there," he said with a Dixie drawl, pointing the way. "Was them crows makin' all that racket."

Arms dangling, the clothed body of a stocky man hung by his only ankle from the cross bar over the left end zone. His right leg was missing, and every-so-often a gutsy crow would land on the corpse and pick at an exposed tendon protruding from the stump. Others circled, waiting their turn. I ran toward the body, waving my fedora and yelling. The crows flew off, taunting me with their "caw, caw!"

Munson and the janitor caught up, each of us doubled over.

Monson wheezed, pointing. "Ain't been dead . . . long as the others . . . There's a ribbon . . . and note."

He was right, even in this heat the guy hadn't begun to putrefy. The janitor puked anyway.

"Cut him down," was all I could manage.

We lowered the body and I went for the familiar note and blue ribbon, retrieving it with my handkerchief. "Our killer's getting lazy," I said, handing the note to my partner, who was too beat to read it and just nodded.

Something about this victim slapped me in the face, another something out of line with our killer's MO: the guy still had his fingers and thumbs. I knelt and lifted a wrist by its shirtsleeve.

"Get a load of this. He's cut or filed-off the fingertips."

"What about teeth?" Munson coughed.

Taking my Scripto from my shirt pocket, I pried open the guy's mouth. "Gone."

"Can I go now?" asked the janitor wiping his mouth with a bandanna, looking pretty spent after barfing for the third time.

I stood. "Yeah, sure. How do we get our car up here?" The janitor pointed north.

"There's a gate, about three-hundred yards yonder. I'll unlock it."

"Thanks," I said, watching the janitor turn and leave. I turned to Munson. "This one's fresh, we need to get him to Cal and fast. I'll stay with the body, you get the car."

Twenty minutes later the janitor pulls up in a Ford pickup under a cloud of dust, the Buick right behind him. "Someone's cut the chain. Damn kids I guess," he said before putting his pickup in gear.

"Hey!" The janitor hit the brakes and leaned out the window.

"Tidrow, the name's Denton Tidrow."

"We'll be in touch, Mr. Tidrow, so keep quiet about what you saw. Understand?"

"Hell, Lieutenant, wouldn't know how to explain it."

The janitor gunned his pickup and washed us in more dust. We watched till the truck disappeared.

Munson spat dry. "Rube."

"Give me a hand."

I unlocked the trunk. We knelt to pick up the body, grunting, hefting, sidestep-ping in unison.

"The note says, 'Getting warmer.' Sounds like Cole wants us to find him," Munson offered.

"For all we know he was giving us a weather report – "

Mid-stride, we dropped the body . . .

"You see what I see?"

Munson nodded, staring down at a pair of narrow tread marks in the dry turf. The tread marks pointed northeast, toward the gate with the cut chain. "I don't think the note was about the weather," he said.

Chapter 8

Cal was running out of limbs to tie the toe tags.

"When did you say you found him?" Colder asked, curiously probing with forceps at the area around the severed knee.

"We got the call around one-fifteen. Janitor says he was on his lunch break when he found him."

"This one's a day old; I'd go as far as to say sometime yesterday afternoon. His blood type is A-B positive, but here's the interesting part." With the tips of his forceps the coroner drew a circle around the outer area of the stump. "Whoever did this used an amputation saw and knew how to use it. The cut is flawless. I reexamined victims one, two and three. Each of their amputations exhibits the same precision. Without a doubt it's your killer's handiwork, but I'd suggest you add mastery of surgical technique to his profile."

Mary Ward sat in the shade at Eco Park, feeding the pigeons, taking discrete slugs from a pint of Old Crow when she thought no one was looking. She had been spending her afternoons this way for the last two weeks since getting her first Social Security check. She no longer needed to stay at the mission, but missed the group and wondered why she hadn't run into any of them lately. A long shadow fell over her pigeons. They scattered, wings beating furiously.

"Hello, Mary."

" – John! I was just thinking about you."

"Were you now? My, you're looking radiant."

"Always mister velvet tongue – Say, you don't look like you're getting much sleep."

"My work."

"That's why I avoid it . . . Sit," Mary said, moving her bags. She patted the readied bench. John sat. "How's the group? Do you see them?"

"They're fine. I see them often."

"I'm glad. I haven't seen them at all."

Cole looked past her, at the bags at the opposite end of the bench. He wanted to change the subject. "Now there's a predicament: two paper bags. I'll bet one holds popcorn, for your pigeons. And the other, a bottle perhaps?"

Suddenly anxious Mary turned, to the source of John's distraction. Carefully, reverently she lifted and offered the bag with the whiskey, as though she were offering her child for sacrifice.

"A friend in need . . ."

"Is a friend indeed Mary. Cheers," Cole toasted.

She followed his every tug on the bottle, making half-hearted raising gestures upward with her open palms.

"Ah," Cole said, wiping his mouth on a shirtsleeve. After appraising her face for the reaction he was after he held out the empty bottle, tipping its neck downward.

Mary let out a whimper.

"Don't look so shocked dear girl, there's more where that came from."

"Where?"

"My lodgings. Not far as the crow flies, and much cooler. Come, we'll raise a glass or two and toast old times."

Relieved, Mary cooed, "Such a smoothie – always knew how to treat a lady." Scooping up her bags, she made an effort to stand but listed. "Whoa!" John caught her. "Spose' I'll need a little help."

"What are friends for?" Cole replied, steadying Mary Ward for the trek northeast.

My Reuben sandwich lay untouched on its yellow-waxed paper, drawing flies. After comparing Cal's reports for the umpteenth time, I slapped my right palm on the open scrapbook.

"Got us a make on victims three and four."

Munson turned from his typewriter, a half-inch of ash dangling from his cigarette.

I pointed to a photo in the scrapbook, of a paunchy guy who looked like he was trying hard to smile about something. "Number three is Sy Talmage, used to pitch for the Cleveland Browns – southpaw, guy with a solid-gold arm and a big gambling-and-losing problem." I thumbed through a pile of press clippings alongside the scrapbook, pulling the one I was after and handing it to Munson. "Mob paid him five grand to tank the final game of the thirty-eight pennant race. After his trial he was banned from baseball – the nineteen-nineteen 'Black Socks' scandal all over."

"Fall from grace," Munson added, crushing his spent cigarette in my overflowing ashtray. "What about number four?"

"Jake Boyle, former head of the I.L.W.U. Bellingham local."

"Caught taking a bribe, too?"

"Yup, to end what looked to be a long strike. Get me last month's 'Missing Persons' file."

"What's up?" Munson asked, moving to the long row of steel file cabinets at the center of headquarters.

"When we found the first victim you said the killing was 'done somewhere private'?"

"That's right."

"Then we won't find John Cole in a house on a street. Our man's held-up somewhere no one can hear the screams of his victims."

Munson set the file on his partner's desk. "So?"

"*So*, what if someone's stumbled on the place before, by accident, and ain't around to tell?"

"Tom, we gotta find number five before the killer does."

"They're bums, Munc, they could be anywhere cause no one cares. We find where he takes them and we find our killer." I opened the thin manila file: "Joey de La Norte, a ten-year old; his parents reported him missing five days ago; he was last seen by his friends, playing in the riverbed off Los Feliz. Donald McDaniel, Water and Power employee: his office reported him missing eleven days ago, after he failed to call in during routine inspection of the aqueducts. They found his truck in Hermosa Beach. Guess what entry shows last on his log?"

"Los Feliz?"

I nodded. "The son-of-a-bitch is holed up in one of the aqueducts off the riverbed."

"There's gotta be a hundred miles of them tunnels."

"Get Water and Power on the phone. Have one of their men meet us on the riverbed at the Los Feliz overpass, someone who knows those tunnels inside-out-and-backwards."

"Right. Say, who's 'number five'?"

"Mary Ward. Used to work for Internal Revenue."

At sixty-seven Fred Ketchum was the oldest man on staff at Water and Power, around when Mulhulland proposed the greatest engineering feat since the Panama Canal. He spread out a map showing the network of underground aqueducts of greater Los Angeles on the hood his Jeep.

"We've got four tributaries along the riverbed near the Los Feliz overpass," Ketchum said, pointing to four symbols on the map that reminded me of smiling cartoon faces you'd see painted on a carnival tent. "Here, here, here, and here; each a quarter-mile apart." Ketchum straightened and pointed. "You can see two of them from here."

I looked across, at the wall of concrete that sloped from the riverbed and ran the length of the channel in either direction. Two inverted archways about ten-feet high were recessed into the concrete berm, each with a spillway that dropped from equal height into the riverbed, the closest one about a hundred yards directly ahead. Heavy iron grating barred anyone from entering the U-shaped aqueducts.

Munson peered through the binoculars. "You'd need a howitzer to blast through."

Ketchum caught my 'what's-up?' stare and shrugged. "You asked for the location of the tributaries, not how a guy could get in."

"Okay, now I'm asking."

Before Ketchum could answer a sandpiper "peeped." We watched it take off from the riverbed and fly east, in the direction of the Los Feliz overpass.

We parked at a Richfield gas station. Ketchum grabbed his toolbox and left his Jeep, climbing into the back of my Buick.

"Streets east of the riverbed are littered with manholes, with smaller aqueducts below that divert runoff. Those are the ones W and P use when we repair the sewers or an underground power line. I suppose with the right tools someone could get down there."

"Let's see that map," I said, reaching over the passenger seat.

Ketchum folded the map in quarters, handing me the section showing the Los Feliz area. He leaned forward, resting his elbows on the seat back.

"Where was McDaniels's last inspection?"

"Here," Ketchum said, pointing to a symbol about a third the size of the spillways along the riverbed. The closest marked street to the symbol was 'Reagent'.

I thought, *Reagent, where've I heard that name?* "What's this, where is it?"

"A tributary, at the north end of a lot bordering the riverbed. The entire block was leveled about a year ago to make way for a hospital. There was a funding snafu and the lot's remained vacant ever since."

"We're five blocks from there," Munson said.

"Let's go." I snatched the mike. "Fifteen to dispatch."

"... Dispatch fifteen. What's your location?"

"Richfield gas station, three-thirteen Los Feliz; en route to eleven-hundred block of Reagent Street. Backup at my command, over."

"... Ten-four fifteen. Out."

The lot was a wasteland of rubble, completely deserted. The few remaining cracker-box houses on Reagent Street were vacant, slated for demolition once the banks hashed out the funding. A stand of Eucalyptus lined the western border of the lot, shielding it from view from the L.A. riverbed, the leaves of the heavy shallow-rooted trees gently rustling in the Santa Ana winds. The only other sounds were the "clicking" of cicadas and an occasional muted horn honk from the direction of Los Feliz Boulevard.

Ketchum pointed the way and we followed, to a concrete culvert running the length of the lot's northern border. The U-shaped culvert was eight-feet deep, with an iron grate barring entrance to a rectangular tunnel at either end. Ketchum's map and toolbox made me feel better. Other than our .38s, a walkie-talkie and flashlight, Munson and I were ill equipped for a journey into the guts of Los Angeles.

"Western duct carries runoff into the riverbed; eastern one leads to a network of tunnels beneath the Los Feliz district," Ketchum said.

I pointed east. "That's where he is."

Munson and I crab-crawled down the gentle slope to the base of the culvert, Ketchum handing down his toolbox before joining us. He took the lead again, to the entrance of the eastern tunnel.

"That's odd," Ketchum said, studying the big, rather new-looking padlock.

"What?"

"Water and Power uses Schlage padlocks. This one's a Yale."

Setting his toolbox down, Ketchum unclipped a ring full of keys and lock picks from his belt, riffling each till he found the ones he wanted. After he'd tried eight of these without success Munson asked, "You sure you can open it?" Ketchum turned slow, pinning him with a hard stare. "I'm sure," he said before squatting to open his toolbox. He then retrieved a thick cobalt bottle with an eyedropper.

"What's that?" I asked.

"Sulfuric acid."

Ketchum carefully began to unscrew the eyedropper, at arm's length not seeming far enough. He pinched then released its bulb till the tube filled with a piss-yellow liquid, its deadly vapor curling as he slowly extracted the eyedropper. Ketchum turned, holding the bottle out to me. Seeing my hesitation he scowled, till I removed the hot vial from his fingertips. With his freed left hand he upended the substituted padlock, as much as its hasp allowed, till its keyhole was almost level. The tip of the eyedropper poised, he carefully moved his right hand into position then, pivoting his wrist in one fluid motion, squirted the stuff into the keyhole. The effect of the acid on the guts of the padlock was quick, Ketchum letting go just before a yellow froth boiled out.

"See that blue-steel lock pick, one I haven't used?"

I bent to pick it up.

"That's the one. Give it here," he gestured.

Yanking a handkerchief from his hip pocket, Ketchum wrapped it around the padlock. He took the lock pick I held out and went to work, quickly jamming it into the keyhole and twisting. There was a brittle "click," and he dropped the corroded padlock and nub of lock pick. After giving Munson and me the 'see-I-told-you-so' look we had coming, he shoved the squeaking grate open and stood aside.

"We can go in now," Ketchum said.

No one offered to take the cobalt bottle from my hands. I let it drop.

Chapter 9

Ketchum's flashlight was bigger than mine.

"I'd understand if you back out now, but we've got a better chance of catching this guy – maybe saving a life – if you show us the way."

"Me, back out on the most exciting thing that's happened since I got laid? C'mon, we're wasting time."

"I'll take point. Munc, you cover our rear. Ketchum, I want you close by, with your map. Let's trade flashlights, yours is brighter." We swapped. I unbuckled my gun-belt, handing Ketchum my backup sidearm. "Ever fire one of these?" He unhooked the keeper and slid the hog leg out of its holster as if he were delivering his own son.

"Um, Colt, .38 Special."

He released its catch and snapped open the cylinder like a pro.

"Dumbdumbs? You guys don't mess around."

"No, Mr. Ketchum, we don't; and from now on neither do you. Keep it holstered unless your life depends on it. In that case, kill the son-of-a-bitch."

We started down the dark tunnel, the damp air reeking of piss and decay. I pressed the thumb button on Ketchum's flashlight and pointed its razor-sharp beam at the ground ahead of me, sweeping. Everything from tires, tin cans, wine bottles, tree limbs, even a brassier, littered the gravel floor. There was a shrill "squeak," then scamper sound, and I swept the flashlight to my left. A rat the size of an eggplant ran the length of the tunnel wall, a smaller one dangling from its mouth.

"Average size rat down here. Cannibalizing their young keeps their population in check."

"Is there anything you don't know, Ketchum?" Munson asked from the rear.

"Yeah, like what women want," Ketchum replied. "Care to shed some light, Lieutenant?"

"Whatever a guy's out of. My ex-wife'll vouch for that . . . This tunnel got a name, a number?"

"Aqueduct thirty-seven. We'll go about three hundred yards before reaching a four-way juncture, the directions are marked at the corners. The north-south one will be larger than this. We'll be under the streets then, get some daylight from the storm drains."

"Any place a guy could call home down here?"

"Sure – least during the summer. They're what W and P call 'stations:' a twelve-square vault with a twenty-five watt bulb – "

The "Yo!" came from behind.

"What've you got, Munc?"

"We're on track," Munson replied, shining his flashlight down at a brown paper bag with 'PROPERTY OF MARY WARD' scrolled in red lipstick. Inside the bag was a shattered pint of Old Crow.

*   *   *

Mary giggled. "Issh's been sssh'well . . . John, but I r-e-a-l-l-y gotta go."

"Long way back to Eco Park old girl."

"No sweat. Gams like mine, girl can always get a ride."

"Show you the way out, perhaps?"

"Got in, didn't I? I'll be oookay, shanks."

"I'm sure you'll be fine."

Screwing up her face, Mary squinted and looked around her host's digs. "This is a tough room. Needs a decorator, cheer it up" she said, letting go her empty glass before keeling over.

Cole sighed. "Party's over."

"This is it," Ketchum announced on reaching the four-way juncture: **NORTH**, **SOUTH**, **EAST**, and **WEST** painted in block letters on the concrete corners.

I checked my Bulova. It read 5:25 p.m. "We've got about three hours of daylight. Which way to the nearest 'station'?"

Ketchum pointed north. "About fifty yards – "

"Quiet," Munson said, holding up a hand . . . "You hear that?"

We listened and caught the faint echo. It seemed to come from the throat of all four aqueducts at once.

"Whistling?"

"'Whistle While You Work,' from Snow White and the Seven Dwarfs," Ketchum answered. Again, he pointed north.

I whispered to Munson, "Try and get Stella on the walkie-talkie. Have her dispatch a unit to the manhole at . . ." Ketchum had the map ready, with his index finger pointing to the intersection . . . "Los Feliz and Victory."

Cole held the taut sash cord to Mary Ward's throat, the feral within him burning, his senses electric. He closed his eyes and began hyperventilating.
I'm truly a necromancer, this netherworld my domain –
The same energy straining to take life sharpened the instinct to protect his own. Cole sniffed the air and listened, then scowled. "Seems we have intruders," he hissed to the woman who lay spread-eagled on the altar, passed out. "You'll be with friends soon," he assured. "But first I must tend to our little interruption."

"What's this?" I asked, pointing to a smaller box on the map that wasn't far from the 'station.'
"A gatehouse," Ketchum answered. "It's where workers divert runoff from one aqueduct to another."
"So he could be in either of these?"
"Sure." Ketchum pointed to six small lines that branched off the main aqueduct. "Or he could be hiding in one of these tributaries, waiting. He already knows we're here, Lieutenant."
"Thanks for sharing that," I said. Munson joined us. "Get through?"
"I'm not sure," Munson answered. "Lot of static down here."
"All right, here's the picture." I indicated to Munson on the map: the two boxes and six branches off the aqueduct. "Our man's held up in one of these, probably with the woman. Ketchum thinks he's on to us."
"You figure he's armed?"
"Count on it," I said.
Ketchum didn't need an invitation. He drew and checked the cylinders of his .38 again.
He caught my look. "You won't need that," I said.
"Then why'd you give it to me?"
"Just leave the police work to us, okay?
Ketchum shrugged and holstered his sidearm.
"Let's go," I said.

From the right wall I swept point up the gauntlet, Ketchum at arm's length behind. Guarding our rear, Munson tried the walkie-talkie again: "Dispatch, unit fifteen." Stella's response was garbled.

"... Go _ head _ _ _teen."

Munson reported: "Proceeding up north aqueduct, towards intersection of Los Feliz and Victory. Suspect, John Cole: white male; six-foot three-inches; one hundred, seventy-eight pounds; brown hair, brown eyes; English accent. Suspect armed and dangerous. May have hostage. Over."

"... Copy ... fif _ _ _ _, dis _ _ _ _ _ out."

Munson slapped the walkie-talkie. "Piece of shit."

The whole scene was creepy, like some medieval dungeon or the catacombs of Rome. Shafts of hard light from the storm drains angled down the course of the aqueduct, traffic drumming overhead. Ketchum tapped my shoulder and pointed to a 'black box' in the wall, to our left and about shoulder-high from the floor. It was big enough for a man to crawl into.

I crossed to the other side, Munson moving up along the right wall, covering me. He nodded. "Clicking"-on Ketchum's flashlight, I thrust the beam into the 'black box,' pivoted then leveled my gun arm. I peered over the rim, expecting a knife in the face. Nothing, the tributary was empty. I waved Munson off and crossed back.

"'Station's' on our right, about twenty yards ahead," Ketchum whispered. "The gate house is ten yards beyond it."

"Why whisper? You said he knows we're here" Munson replied, unwrapping and stuffing three sticks of Beemans into his mouth.

"Nervous I guess," Ketchum answered.

We moved ahead in the same formation, only tighter ...

*   *   *

Crouched before the entrance to the 'station,' I listened. Not a peep. Taking a two-by-two mirror from my shirt pocket, I held out my other hand to Munson.

"Give me that gum."

Munson handed over the wad from his mouth. I stuck the gum on the handle of Ketchum's flashlight and pressed the back of the mirror to it. Pivoting my wrist and angling the mirror gave me a clear view inside: a mattress, GI blankets, some books, canned food, a Sterno stove, empty liquor bottles, candles, and two campaign chairs. Even from this side of the wall it smelled like a tomb.

"No one's home. I'm going in."

.38 drawn, my back to the jamb, I cross-stepped in and swept the perimeter. Satisfied the place was empty, I turned to leave. There, adjacent to the doorway, was a red wagon; above the wagon, written in blood on the wall, the words **LOOKING FOR ME?**

Mike McCune

Chapter 10

Ten yards made a big difference: flies now as thick as the odor of formaldehyde. I crouched before the entrance to the gatehouse and used the mirror again. Nothing could have prepared me for the sight.

"It's a slaughterhouse in there, he's got body parts hanging everywhere... There's a woman – in one piece. She's on a concrete slab, not moving."

"Cole?" Munson asked.

I pivoted the mirror. "Clear." Munson drew his .38 and slid past me into the gatehouse, moving to the woman. "Stay sharp," I said to Ketchum then followed my partner in.

Munson placed two fingertips on the woman's left carotid artery. "She's alive."

For the first time in my life, I was scared. The instant it took to glance down at the woman I could see the killer had toyed with her. There were razor cuts on her face and arms, and faint bruising on her throat indicating he'd started to strangle her but had stopped. She smelled like a distillery.

Munson shook the woman. "C'mon lady, wake up."

"Someone's whistling Disney tunes again," Ketchum announced from the other side of the entrance.

"Where from?" I asked.

"Can't tell, but I'd feel a lot better holding a gun out here."

*   *   *

Mary's head pounded like a bowling alley, but it was her throat she reached for. She could barely swallow, opening her eyes not much easier. Even through the haze she could tell the face staring down at her wasn't John's, yet had the strangest feeling this was a good thing.

"Who the hell are you? Where am I?"

"Munson. I'm a detective."

Beyond the stranger's face Mary could almost make out: floating arms, legs, and torsos? She pointed at the apparitions. "What's with the mannequins?" She cupped her hands over her eyes to stop the room from swimming. "Boy, have I got the swirls."

"Get up," Munson said, bending the woman upright from the shoulders.

I dropped our cover and moved to help her find the floor. "What's your name?"

"Mary Ward." Mary lowered her hands, shook her head and blinked, till her eyes focused on the other face now staring at her. "Who're you?"

"Lieutenant Dreyfus – "

"Oh my God, they're real! They're dead!" Mary covered her mouth to keep from puking.

"That whistling is getting louder!" Ketchum called, peering in from around the entrance. "Holy shit!"

Munson and I half-dragged the woman past Ketchum. Back in the aqueduct we heard the creepy 'Whistle-While-You-Work' tune, it seeming to come from everywhere and nowhere. It got on our nerves.

Sirens and gunning engines suddenly passed overhead, then rubber "screeching" to a halt not far beyond. We'd got through.

"Get her out of here," I said to Munson and Ketchum. I watched as they helped drag Mary Ward toward Victory, heard the "clang" of a manhole cover and saw the shaft of hard light that spelled freedom . . .

"Just you and me, Lieutenant." The voice seemed to come in a three-hundred-and-sixty degree echo. Or was it in my head? I turned, facing west: nothing but a corridor fading to darkness.

"Cole?"

"The juncture, Lieutenant . . . Come alone . . . Hurry, or you'll be late for our rendezvous."

It couldn't have been more personal. I ran, full tilt, back down the aqueduct toward the four-way juncture, Munson calling after me, "Hey, Tom, where're you going?"

"You're getting warmer, Lieutenant. I can almost feel your jugular pounding."

The voice was as soft and deep as a junkie's lullaby, but I didn't answer. My back skimming the north wall, I swept the vault with my .38, my gun hand shaking, thinking *I'm chasing a ghost.* "Cole?"

There was a "whoosh" and my hands were suddenly too busy to hold a gun, groping frantically instead for my throat. I was being lifted off the ground by an unseen force, my heels kicking at the wall, gasping, going bug-eyed. It's amazing how acute your senses become when you're being strangled.

"Welcome to my world, Lieutenant."

I had a reply in mind but couldn't find the words. Reaching up and back, into the wall as far as my arms could without breaking, I found what felt like a collar, grabbing hold and yanking forward with all my strength. I fell hard, something heavy falling almost on top of me then "shuffling" to recover, only faster. My eyes went spastic trying to spot my gun. I tried to stand. There was another "whoosh" and I turned too late to feel a sharp pain across my right shoulder, blood flowing from a deep cut. Dazed and unable to strike back, I instinctively raised my arms to shield my face.

Cole brandished the bloodied scalpel, sneering like a wolf. "End game, Lieutenant, say your prayers. Any last words or final moral obligation, some ethical code?"

"What, to end a sick fuck like you? Absolutely."

"Bold as brass for someone bleeding to death – "

"Drop the knife!"

Cole turned. "Ah, detective Munson – the second-stringer," he said before lunging at his prey.

A "pop" echoed off the cold concrete, and something warm and wet that wasn't mine splattered across my face, the phantom dropping in front of me, making gurgling sounds. I couldn't help thinking, *good shot*. And that's when nothing choked or cut me anymore, or talked back smart, when I felt okay enough just to collapse, pass out and let someone else deal with it. I remember muttering to myself, "Vacation. I need a vacation."

Made in the USA
Charleston, SC
06 April 2014